SAVING THE KING

A KING'S TALE

LEILANI LOVE

Copyright © 2018 by Leilani Love

All rights reserved.

No part of this book may be reproduced in any form or by any electronic or mechanical means, including information storage and retrieval systems, without written permission from the author, except for the use of brief quotations in a book review.

❦ Created with Vellum

*I want to thank my family and friends.
You guys are amazing and I am blessed to have you in my life.*

*I also want to say a special Thank You to Scott C. and Susan P. For
helping me with this book.*

ALSO BY LEILANI LOVE

The Dragon Ruby Series
Violca's Dragon
The King's Fire
Violca's Vow
Kassandra's Wolf
Warrick's Hope
Ally's Guard

CHAPTER 1

With one hand on the seat and the other trying to keep the crying baby tight to her chest, Katrina watched out the window, the world seemed to be flying past them. The snow, which had started to fall earlier, was now coming down thicker as the sound of the thunder grew louder and closer.

Katrina felt each bump and her bottom hurt as the carriage hit each rut in the road at a pace much faster than was expected. She made a soothing noise to the baby, not sure if she was trying to comfort him or herself. As they quickly rounded a corner, she felt the carriage begin to tip under her. Before it completely flipped on its side, she did the only thing she could think of; she let go of the seat and wrapped her arms around the baby to protect it from the inevitable crash.

As the carriage toppled she felt herself landing against the window, crying out as it continued to slide along the road for what felt like several long minutes. Dazed and a little confused, she was almost surprised when the carriage door flew open and the guard that she'd seen riding behind them reached down to help her out. "Hurry, they're right behind us!"

Katrina scrambled to a standing position, so she could hand

him the baby. When she reached out her hand, she remembered the baby bag and milk and grabbed it before letting the guard pull her out.

"What happened?" she started to ask, looking around realizing that the horses that were pulling the carriage were gone. She knew that, despite it feeling like they slid forever, she doubted they'd slid more than a few feet.

"Milady, quickly. On my horse. Morgana's men are right behind us," he answered pulling her along with him. He held the baby with one arm as he pushed his free arm out to give her a quick boost. Once she was upon the horse, he'd handed her the baby and started to mount behind her when she noticed shadows coming up behind them. Through the trees the sound of female laughter emulated, almost as if it were being carried by the wind.

"Ride, Milady! Stay on the road and head straight back to the castle." With that she watched as he smacked the horse's hindquarters telling the horse to go on without him. Leaning forward on the horse she glanced over her shoulder as the shadowy figures came out of the trees attacking the guard. His loud battle cry was the last thing she heard before they surrounded him.

Scared, she urged the horse faster as she noticed different figures in the woods keeping up with her. The sound of thunder startled her. What she'd thought was thunder was a giant shadow of riders coming up behind her. With it snowing, there was very little light, and she couldn't make them out. All she could see was that they were catching up.

The figures on the left started to come through the woods. The horse had red eyes that shone brightly in the night, and the rider seemed to be covered in black markings. He wore no shirt, just a pair of brown leather pants. His grin exposed teeth that had been sharpened to points, causing her to shudder. When she felt something hit her on the side she cried out, squeezing the baby tighter as someone tried to bump her off the horse.

Katrina adjusted herself as the horse started to veer and she used her legs, encouraging the poor horse to go faster. When she was bumped again, Katrina felt the horse almost slip. She knew if he was bumped a third time they would probably stumble. With a prayer to the gods for help, she pulled the reins, forcing the horse off the road and into the woods.

Katrina felt a moment of reprieve until she saw the first arrow fly past her head. She stayed low as she tried to weave between trees, when she felt something slice her arm. Katrina bit her lip to keep from crying out in pain and hoped that they didn't get any closer.

There was nowhere to hide, and Katrina heard the baby begin to cry in her arms. She wished she could comfort him, but her focus had to be on getting them out of there. When she noticed a large hill ahead she found herself hoping they could just get there.

Without any warning, the horse stumbled, and she felt him pitch forward. Her instinct to protect the baby kicked in and she let go of the reins as they were sent flying over the horse's head. Landing hard on her side, she felt the wind being knocked out of her. There were several arrows sticking out of the poor horse and he let out a soft whine.

Stunned, it took her several minutes to raise her body so sore it protested as she tried to stand. She looked down at the bag she was carrying. Not sure what else to do, she opened it up and slid the baby on top of the bladder of the milk. Arthur was just small enough to fit. The bag should help keep out some of the cold as she carried him in the woods.

"Shhh, my little prince. You just have to be brave a little longer." With that she flipped the top of the bag back over to cover him from the elements and put the strap of the bag over her head. This would at least free up both of her hands and make it easier to run. She felt a twinge of guilt for carrying the future prince this way but knew that her first obligation was to protect him and that would be easier with the use of her hands.

The hill was still ahead of her, which meant the possibility of a cave and Katrina ran toward it. The horses coming up behind her made the ground shake, and she fought the urge to look back, knowing it would just slow her down. Weaving around trees she stumbled, her soft leather boots offering no protection from the snow.

Coming up on both sides, the horses started to surround her, and Katrina felt a deep fear of what was to come. Almost tripping over a big branch, she grabbed onto it hoping if she could at least fight them off then maybe, just maybe, the gods would answer her prayers.

She heard chuckling as the men got off the horses. She noticed all of them had those black markings on their chests and faces. Despite the cold, not one wore a shirt and they all seemed unfazed by the frigid air as they started to close in around her. Swinging the stick around she yelled, "Stay back!"

The chuckling got louder, and she heard one speak in a language she'd never heard before. Based on their faces she could tell that whatever it was they were saying, she would not like it. "I am one of the Queen's ladies. Attacking me is an assault on the Queen…"

The laughter grew and one of the men stepped closer to her. He was a giant of a man, and when Katrina swung the stick in her hand and it hit him, she regretted it instantly. The look of pure anger and hatred in his eyes made her legs quiver. Katrina felt herself shrink as she realized she hadn't hurt him at all but instead made him even angrier.

As he raised his arm to hit her the sound of growling filled the air. She turned just in time to see a big white wolf land on his back. As the men changed their focus from her to the wolves, Katrina did the only thing she could think of, she picked up her skirt and ran.

Without knowing what direction to go, she kept heading toward the hill. She was cold and exhausted and could still hear the men yelling behind her, along with the sound of at least two wolves.

The hill didn't seem to get any closer as she ran. As it got colder and colder, Katrina felt herself stumbling. Each step took more and more energy until she finally fell. The baby's cries had turned into soft whimpers and Katrina held him close as she gave in to the desire to lie down for a moment. As her eyes started to close she wasn't sure if she saw a large white figure approaching or if her mind was just playing tricks on her.

CHAPTER 2

Most of the men had taken off in a run after the wolves started attacking. There were four in the pack, total. The two brothers Bryan rescued as pups and their mates. Snow, the biggest and the alpha of the group, had attacked the man who was about to strike the woman. After that, the other three attacked. Most the men who resembled demons with their markings took off.

Bryan took note of which way the woman ran before he used his bow to shoot one of the men who'd tried to follow her. Once the arrow flew, several of the men who weren't already fleeing, turned toward him, swords raised. Several of them were far enough away that he was able to take aim and shoot some arrows at them. Bryan dropped his bow and pulled the sword from its sheath just in time to block the first blow. Face to face with his attacker, the only things between them were two swords pressing against each other. The man's eyes were dark, and Bryan noticed the black markings all over his face were in an odd pattern. Demon was the first thought that crossed Bryan's mind.

Bryan was tall, but this man was taller. Bigger did not mean smarter. He knew he couldn't overpower him, so he pushed forward, hard. When he felt the guy push back, he moved quickly to the left, taking a step that caused the demon man to fall, and giving him time to slice his sword and stab him in back.

As he ducked into position to defend the next attack, he saw one of the female wolves, Minx, jump up and attack a man. A glance around showed him that almost all the men had fled, and Snow was no longer there. Neither was the giant man he'd attacked earlier.

Bryan picked up the bow as he jogged to where he had last seen the woman. From the tracks he saw, the woman had gone one way, while the man who had been holding her went another. Snow had followed the woman. Bryan knew his wolf wouldn't hurt her, but he wanted to make sure he got to her before the cold did. The woman already appeared exhausted and her dress and cloak would not protect her from the elements.

The three wolves walked with him, as he followed the pack alpha and the trail of the female who had run away. With the snow still falling, both their trails were practically gone, but the wolves next to him let him know which way to go. Bryan started to wonder if they'd wandered too far, when the sound of a baby crying caught his attention. Did the woman have a baby with her?

When he finally found Snow, he was lying tucked against the woman on the ground. Bryan hurried over and saw that the woman had a bag nestled against her and that the crying sound was coming from within. As he picked her up, pulling her against him, he noticed how cold she was and realized that Snow's heat had probably kept her from freezing to death.

Before standing, he adjusted the bag so that when he picked her up, it would stay nestled against her, giving both her and the baby some warmth. He needed to get them both to shelter as quickly as he could. Bryan sent up a prayer as he hastily walked back the way they'd come. The woman and baby in his arms barely weighed a thing, and when the baby started to quiet down, he felt himself hurrying faster. "Come on, little one, just a bit longer."

Once he got to the horses, he carefully mounted his, pulling his packhorse closer. He had gone hunting and had extra furs. He picked the thickest one he could find and tucked it around the woman. As he looked down at her for the first time, he noticed how pale her skin was. Her blond hair, clinging to the side of her face, was wet from the snow. She was so small in his arms. He wanted to check on the infant, but with the weather as it was, he decided their best option was to get him back to his cabin fast and get them both warm.

He rode as quickly as he could. Bryan's home was about half a day's ride from Camelot or any other major village. Bryan chose it because he loved the quiet. He was more comfortable here in the woods. Normally, riding alone brought him peace, but as he began to worry about the two in his arms he wished his home was closer. When the baby quit fussing, he started to worry. Bryan found himself hoping that the baby was just tired from crying and had fallen asleep.

When Bryan saw his stone cabin appear he whispered, "Just a bit farther." Since he had gone to check on his traps and knew he would be gone for a long period of time, he had killed the fire.

The horse had barely come to a stop when Bryan hopped off, kicking open the door so he could get them inside. Entering his room, he set them both on his bed, choosing to light the fire before checking on them.

He opened the bag, surprised at how small the baby was. Not sure if it was a girl or boy, all he knew was that the baby couldn't be more than a few days old. The leather of the bag should have kept out most of the wind, but he wondered what had possessed the woman to take the baby out in this weather. He was a little cold but not nearly as cold as the woman on the bed. Her body heat and bag had shielded the baby from the harshest part of the winter weather.

The woman's dress was wet, and he quickly removed her soft leather boots before attempting the gown that clung to her. Bryan turned her to her side to untie the laces on the back. Finding the strings wet and knotted, he grabbed the knife from his belt and cut them, loosening the dress enough to pull it up and over her head. Removing the rest of her soaked clothes, he tucked her into the bed putting extra furs over her to try and help warm her.

The fire was not intense enough to warm up the room, let alone his nearly frozen guests, so Bryan did the only thing he could think of and stripped out of his clothes. As he crawled under the blankets, he pulled the woman close and put the baby on his chest. Her body was ice-cold, and based on how little her chest moved, she was barely breathing.

The woman was tiny, her hips and flat stomach were not that of a woman who had just given birth to this baby. Bryan couldn't help but wonder who she was and how it was she came to be carrying a new baby in a bag. He also wondered about the painted-men who had attacked them. Would they be coming back to get her and the babe?

The infant warmed up the fastest and fell asleep on his chest. Bryan was careful, having had some experience with newborn babies. He moved the child to the other side of the female who was still icy cold, her lips blue. He worried what would happen if he didn't warm her up soon.

Bryan pulled the woman closer to him, wrapping his arms around her and rubbing her back. At first, she was so still he worried he was too late and sent up a prayer. When she started to shake a bit in his arms, he said a small prayer of thanks.

As he held her close, he brushed her wet hair back from her face. She was tiny compared to him; her features were delicate. He picked up her hand and rubbed it with one of his. Her soft hands told him she was a lady, which raised more questions about who she and the baby that she had carried with her were.

Bryan fell asleep holding the mystery woman in his arms, waking up when the baby started to fuss next to them. Not sure how long he had been sleeping, Bryan got up, picking up the baby. As the child let out a cry, he searched the room for the bag that he'd been in, with the hopes of finding the babies supplies. Finding both a changing cloth and a bladder of milk, he carried them into the living room.

It had been a long time since he had changed a baby; he hoped he hadn't forgotten. The wolves got up from where they were laying to check out the small human making so much noise. Picking up the shirt, he tried to figure out how the ties were set up before removing the cloth. The baby pulled up his legs and let out a loud cry, his fists flailing in protest.

"Shh, little one. I'm just trying to remember how to put this thing back on you."

The baby continued to cry, his face going red in protest. "Aww little laddie, we will get you all dry and fed," Bryan said, as he quickly removed one cloth napkin out from under him to put on a clean one. His first attempt failed miserably, but the second one stayed on well enough.

When the little lad started sucking on his hand and whimpering, Bryan realized he needed to find a way to feed him. Bryan held the baby as he examined the bladder of milk. He had seen something like it once before and remembered that a father had made a similar bag to use to feed the animals when their mothers were not able to produce enough milk.

"Here you go little laddie, it's all right." After several attempts, the baby finally latched on and started sucking on the corner of the bag. He sighed in relief. The male wolves lay back down as the two females lay next to him still curious about the little human. Minx, Snow's female, had given birth a year ago, but the pup did not survive. She put her paw on his lap, her motherly instincts kicking in.

"Minx if you want a pup of your own, you need to bother

Snow. This one is not for you." She huffed before standing up and licking his face. When he laughed, she finally left his side to go lie with Snow.

Once the little lad was fed, Bryan noticed he had fallen back to sleep. Not sure what to do with him now, he put the baby on his bed in order to free his arms to make a makeshift bed of furs. He wanted to make sure the baby stayed warm, and the bedroom was the easiest room to do that. Setting up a pile of furs in the corner of the floor, Bryan moved the baby to the new, makeshift bed.

Bryan went to the bed to check on the sleeping woman. Her lips were no longer blue, instead a film of sweat had appeared on her forehead. Bryan reached out touching her head. She was burning up. Fevers were tricky. As a lad, his mother had taught him that it was best to keep a feverish person wrapped up in blankets and bathe them often.

His sister had just had a baby and would not be visiting until the weather cleared. He would have liked her help with the baby and caring for the woman, but he knew she already had enough on her hands. Plus, Thomas was very protective. He would never let his wife leave the house in the snow just after having their baby.

"I need you to get better quickly, lassie. I'm sure the little lad would much prefer you to take care of him than me. Plus, I don't believe he's yours, and his mum and pa are probably worried about him," Bryan said, as he gently pushed her hair back from her face.

The lad raised a lot of questions. He didn't appear big enough to be taken from his mother and the woman before him, with her small waist and flat stomach, couldn't have given birth. How did she end up with him? Were there more people that needed help right now who were attacked by those marked up men? Did she kidnap him? So many questions, none of which would be answered until she woke up.

CHAPTER 3

Katrina felt smothered and so hot. She tried to kick off the blankets that were on her and growled in frustration when they seemed to magically reappear. Hearing an unfamiliar male voice telling her that she needed to stay covered, made her kick her legs again, determined to kick off the blankets.

"What a stubborn little lass you are," she heard with a small chuckle.

She wanted to open her eyes and see who this voice belonged to but couldn't seem to work up enough energy. As she started to fall back to sleep, she wondered where she was and had a nagging feeling she was forgetting something.

They were chasing her. Men with markings were chasing her, as she held her bag tightly to her. The baby was crying, and she had to get away. No matter which way she ran, they seemed to find her. She let out a scream when she tripped. When she fell, it felt like they'd covered her with nets pinning her to the ground.

Katrina's eyes flew open, and she screamed again seeing a pair of dark brown eyes above her. The sound of a baby crying made her panic more. Trying to stand, she felt him pushing her down. "What have you done with him? Where is Arthur?"

She felt him put something cool on her forehead, as he made a soothing noise that confused her. "Shh, the lad is just fine. You just woke him up."

She tried to get up again, as the panicky feeling clawed at her. As he pushed her back, she felt him put something heavy on her chest, and he continued to wipe her forehead with something wet and cool. She wanted to protest but couldn't seem to gain the strength to move or fight him. Her eyes closed, and she gave in to the need to let sleep overtake her.

As soon as she fell back asleep, Bryan went to the baby to pick him up. When she screamed, Minx had gotten up and run in to the room, going to the crying baby. Minx nudged him and stayed with the baby, calming him down while Bryan talked to the woman who had apparently been having a nightmare. She had been having several over the last few days, causing him to learn a few things. First, whoever she was to the baby, she believed she was in charge of protecting him. He still hadn't learned her name, but at least he could stop calling the baby lad and instead call him Arthur.

When he was sure she had fallen back to sleep, Bryan took the baby into the front room. "Arthur," Bryan said, watching as the baby tried to suck on his fist, letting him know he was hungry again. "A strong name for a strong, little lad. Let's get you fed, so that you can grow into it."

Bryan had gotten into a routine with the baby and the woman. The baby was simple; he wanted to be fed and cleaned, and when he wasn't sleeping, which was often, he wanted a bit of attention. Minx often checked in on him, and little Arthur seemed to enjoy it. The woman, he tried to bathe in warm water in an attempt to get her temperature down, saying a silent prayer that her fever would break soon. He kept her warm and sat with her sometimes at night when the house was quiet, and he wondered about her. Sometimes, when she awoke from a nightmare, she would look at him, her eyes glazed, screaming about Merlin, or the painted men. He had met the wizard twice before, and he wondered how it was that this woman had come to know him.

Other times, her eyes focused on him. Those times she let things slip. He tried to ask her what her name was, but she never answered him.

When Arthur was fed and changed, Bryan smiled at how easy it had become to change the baby's clothes since the first time. Bryan was impressed with himself.

A yawn escaped him, and he lay on the pile of furs. He had created himself a makeshift bed since the woman had taken up residence in his. He felt protective of her and chose to sleep on the floor next to the bed. This kept him in position to watch over her and the baby. So far, there had been no signs of the men who had been chasing her. The wolves had gone out regularly. Bryan knew that the wolves would most likely keep anything from getting too close to the home. If they managed to get past the wolves, they would be in trouble.

Bryan listened to the woman above him sleeping soundly. Her breath was even, telling him that she was in a deep sleep and wasn't presently plagued by nightmares. He hated that she was troubled in dreams, but until she awoke, he couldn't think of how to help her.

Bryan's mind wandered for a bit before he finally fell asleep. His dreams were haunted by the mysterious woman in his bed who had appeared so suddenly in his life.

The sound of the baby making little happy noises woke him up. He rolled to the side to see Snow leaning over the baby, tickling him with his fur. He smiled, out of all the wolves during the day, the big male appeared to be bored with the baby. It was nice to see the old guy more interested than he appeared. After a minute, Snow took a step back and gave him a look that made him laugh out loud.

"Too bad, old dog, I saw you playing with the baby," Bryan said, as he got up to check on the little lad. He patted Snow on the head before picking up the baby, "What do you think, Snow? Does he look like an Arthur?"

He fed and changed the baby before laying him on the floor, on the rug. Arthur was an easy baby with the help of the wolves who often seemed to like to lie next to him. Snow, pretending indifference, walked to the corner of the room to lie down. "You're already caught, Snow. You can lay with him."

Snow huffed and put his head on his paws. When he laughed, he noticed how Arthur was startled by the noise. He had so many questions about Arthur. There was a cut on his hand that, even though he thought the baby was young, was totally healed and a mark on his backside. It reminded Bryan of a brand marking, but that was ridiculous, right? Branding a baby was barbaric, and if that was the case, did the woman in his bed steal him from the men he had saved them from.

They had gotten into a bit of a routine. After he fed and changed the baby, he put him on the rug and watched him. Besides crying, the baby had a few sounds that he interpreted to mean the baby was happy. He didn't stay awake very long, and he ate often. Bryan smiled down at him thinking that if the baby kept eating like he was, he would grow up quickly.

When Arthur started to fuss, he picked him back up and walked him around the room, until he felt him fall back to sleep. Taking him back to the room, he laid him in his bed. Since he wasn't sure how long they were going to be here, he started making a bed for him. The wood already cut, Bryan spent the little bit of time he had carving everything in the living room. Bryan had a small farm for his food, and animals, but traded mostly in furs and his woodworking. The bed would be finished in a day, two, max, if the woman or infant needed his attention more than normal.

He sighed, glancing at the door to his room. The woman in his bed was beautiful, and he had a hard time believing that she, or the baby, would not be missed. She was stunning and based on her soft skin and fine clothes, she was a highborn lady. That came with another set of problems. If he got caught with her in his bed, her reputation would be ruined. He would have dressed her, but with the continued baths and making sure her needs were met, it was just easier not to worry about putting something on and off.

It had been more than ten days since he'd brought her home, and Bryan was just starting to think he was about to lose her when her fever finally broke. She hadn't awoken yet, but when he found her covered in sweat, he gave her a warm bath. A sigh of relief escaped him, as he glanced down at the baby in his arms. "Arthur, the little lass is going to pull through."

The baby made a noise, and he laughed, "I'm happy about that too."

Arthur was strong, and the two of them had formed a bond of sorts. He seemed to understand that Bryan had no idea what to do with him, besides feeding and changing him. He helped his mother and his sister with his nephew but never for a full day. The rest of his baby experience came from the animals he had raised. Besides his three horses, he had several pigs, cows and goats. He didn't count the chickens, since he never really did anything with them after they had hatched.

Bryan knew it was best to feed the baby before he even attempted to take care of the woman in his bed. As good as Arthur was, he definitely didn't appreciate having his breakfast pushed back. When Arthur scrunched up his face letting him know he was going to express his unhappiness with the situation,

Bryan chuckled. "I got you some fresh milk this morning, no need to throw a fit."

He didn't want to leave her alone but knew better than to wait. As he sat in the chair feeding him the milk, Bryan thought about the baby in his arms. Every day, he seemed to get just a bit stronger. He wondered how long it would be until he started holding his own head up or trying to walk. An image of him trying to chase the wolves around made him smile. "I have a funny feeling you're going to be a handful when you get bigger."

The wolves had left this morning to go on a hunt and the house felt empty. It had been snowing for a few days and the wolves were eager to go out for a run, making the house feel quieter than normal. The baby fed, he took him with him into the room.

As he laid Arthur in the bed, Bryan smiled. "Soon we will find your parents. They must be worried about you."

Bryan had brought in a basin of water and a cloth earlier before the baby had demanded his attention. There was something compelling about the woman in his bed. The few times she had opened her eyes, she had been in the middle of a nightmare, and he couldn't make sense of what she had been trying to say. She seemed to be mad at Merlin and frightened of the demon men who were chasing her. She had asked him about the baby several times, even asking if he was an angel sent to protect them. Bryan had chuckled thinking his sister would have laughed at hearing him being called an angel.

A hand reached out and grabbed his as her clear, golden-brown eyes opened and met his for the first time. "Where is Arthur? Is he safe?"

CHAPTER 4

Katrina awoke to find herself staring into a pair of dark brown eyes. She knew she didn't know him, but she recognized his face. His long, dark hair hung just past his shoulders. Even though he needed a shave, she couldn't deny how handsome he was. He had a strong jawline and full lips that looked like they were meant for sin.

His lips curved into a smile and she blushed, wondering if he'd read her thoughts. "You're finally awake, lass."

She tried to sit up, her body shaking. When the cold air hit her chest, Katrina glanced down to realize she was naked. Panic overtook her, as she used the blanket to try and cover herself. "Who are you? Where are my clothes?" she asked him, as a panicky feeling began to overtake her.

The man took a small step back and put his hand up. She had a funny feeling he meant to be comforting. "Easy, lass you're safe. I found you and the little one out in the snow. Do you remember being attacked in the woods?"

Katrina nodded and whispered, "I remember. Where's Arthur? Where's the baby?"

She watched him move and noticed a small bed close to hers.

She watched as he reached into the bed and picked up the baby. Letting out a sigh of relief, she forgot about her modesty and reached out her arms to hold him. The man smiled putting Arthur in her arms. "He is a good lad. Only really fusses when he wants something."

Katrina held him close, as she kept an eye on the man. The room was dark but warm. She noticed that the room had its own fireplace. The bed was big and stuffed with feathers, but his clothes were plain. A simple linen work shirt and a pair of leather britches. He wasn't poor, but he definitely was not a lord.

"Thank you for taking care of him," she said watching the baby in his arms. "How long have we been here?"

"Ten days," the man told her. She took note of the way he watched her. "Why were those men attacking you?"

Katrina looked away from Arthur and up at the man. She didn't know for sure, but she had a funny feeling those were Morgana's men. "I don't know."

He raised one eyebrow at her. Her cheeks heated up and she looked away. "Thank you for helping us. We were going to Camelot. I appreciate all your help, but I need to get him back."

"Arthur's parents are in Camelot?"

She nodded touching Arthur's cheek and he made a soft sound. "His parents left before me. I need to get him back to them."

He nodded, and she got the feeling that he didn't totally believe her. "Your body is probably weak from the fever. You will need a few days before you can travel. I'm going to make you some stronger broth than what I've been giving you. I wouldn't get up just yet."

Katrina nodded, adjusting the blankets again. "Thank you."

She watched him start to walk out of the room and called out, stopping him. "What is your name?"

"Bryan," he said over his shoulder.

Katrina watched him walk out of the room. He was a big man.

She noticed his doorway was taller than most, so he wouldn't have to stoop down. The baby moved in her arms, and she smiled down at him. "Hello, my little prince," Katrina said.

When Katrina was tasked with taking the baby, she'd felt annoyed. She was one of the Queen's personal ladies in waiting. A close friend to the Queen shouldn't have to do menial tasks like running an errand, but when she'd awoken and thought she'd lost the baby... Katrina had never felt so panicked. There was a sense of relief when Bryan had picked up the baby, and she saw that he was safe.

"Has Bryan been taking good care of you?" When the baby squirmed in her arms, she carefully put him down next to her. Despite being asleep for a few days she, realized she was tired. She turned on her side and watched as Arthur made little faces and cooing noises.

The smell of beef hit her, and she felt her stomach grumble. As she put her head back down on her pillow, she found herself hoping she could keep her eyes open long enough to eat. With her hand on the baby, she started to feel her eyes close as sleep pulled her under.

Not sure how long she'd slept, Katrina awoke to find herself alone in the bed. Arthur was no longer lying near her. She could hear the soft sound of breathing near her. She moved over to the edge and looked down to see Bryan lying atop a pile of furs.

Without his questioning gaze, she was able to study him. He was tall, broad-shouldered, and his long, dark hair had just the hint of a curl to it that made her want to touch it. Besides being tall, he was also muscular. The fire in the room gave her just enough light that she could trace his muscles. His blanket was low on his hips, and her eyes followed the muscle on his stomach all the way down.

His chest wasn't the first naked one she had ever seen, but it was the only one she couldn't seem to pull her eyes away from. Katrina fought the urge to reach down and touch him before some movement caught her eye making her jump and forcing her gaze back up to his face. His eyes were open and staring at her. Her entire face felt hot as he smiled up at her. "You look hungry, lass. Can I get you something to eat?"

Katrina started to shake her head when her stomach grumbled at the thought of something inside it. With only the light from the fire, she was sure he couldn't know what she had been thinking about. He chuckled softly, and when he stood up, she found herself a little disappointed that he was wearing a pair of soft leather pants that were unlaced and hung low on his waist.

She pretended to busy herself, as she adjusted herself in bed. She tried to sit up and was surprised when he gently slid his arm under her back to help her up. He adjusted the pillows, so she could sit up on her own and lean on them. Katrina held the blanket up making sure she stayed covered, even as she realized he had seen her naked.

"Thank you," Katrina whispered, as she noticed the faint shadow of hair growth on his strong jawline.

Bryan turned to look at her, his face so close to hers that she had to fight the urge to reach out and touch his cheek. He was handsome enough, that if she had seen him inside the castle, she would have noticed him. She would never have talked to him though. As the Queen's lady-in-waiting, he would have never been allowed close to her.

"What's your name, lass?" Bryan asked, as he straightened up.

Katrina opened her mouth to tell him it was Lady Armstrong, when she realized she didn't really know who he was. Was he indeed her rescuer? "Katrina," she said, deciding at this point, telling him her first name wouldn't put them in any more danger.

"Katrina," he repeated with a smile.

Her name on his lips sent a shiver down her spine. He left her then, to think about her reaction to him. The house was quiet.

She could hear him moving around in the other room. In a few minutes, he came back with a big wooden bowl in his hands.

When she reached out to grab the bowl, he shook his head. "No, let me. You're still very weak."

Realizing he was right, she nodded. She watched as he gathered a spoonful. "I kept it over a low fire. It is warm but not hot," he said, as he brought the spoon to her mouth.

Katrina opened her mouth dutifully feeling like a small child. She couldn't even remember the last time she hadn't fed herself. It smelled wonderful, and when he fed her that first spoonful, she was pleasantly surprised at how good it tasted. She moaned softly, smiling at him. "It's delicious."

He sent her a small smile and continued feeding her. The room was so quiet that the soft crackle of the fire in the hearth was the only sound in the room. Katrina kept from staring at his bare chest and instead examined the room. The bed was big, several trunks were lining the wall. She was surprised to see there was even a window, with glass. Glass was expensive, which made her even more curious about the man feeding her.

Despite how hungry she was, she was full after just a few bites. When he raised another spoonful, she shook her head. "No, thank you. I don't think I could eat another bite."

He nodded putting down the spoon. "You ate more tonight than you have been," Bryan said with a look of understanding.

She nodded, realizing she needed to relieve herself. "I umm..." she stammered a bit unsure how to ask. She didn't want to think about the fact that this man had been taking care of all of her needs for the last ten days.

Bryan frowned before a look crossed his face. "Let me grab you one of my shirts, and I will help you."

Bryan went to one of the drawers lining the walls, and after a bit of searching brought her a shirt. It was a simple white shirt and after he handed it to her, he turned around to let her put it on. She could smell him on it. He smelled woodsy and manly.

After she was covered, she cleared her throat to let him know she was finished. Bryan reached out to help her up and hold her steady, as she felt her legs shake under her. Her legs felt weak, yet they firmly held her up, so she took a step to test her strength. Bryan's arm around her waist was the only thing that kept her from falling.

"Lean on me," Bryan said close to her ear. "Your legs aren't yet strong enough, but soon."

He carried her out of the bedroom and into the main room. The house was open and clean. When he got to a door, he helped her open it, and it led to a bathroom. He handed her a candle to give her light and after he left to give her privacy, she used the wall to help keep from falling.

When she was finished, she leaned against the wall next to the door and opened it. With her legs shaking, she took a step forward only to feel them quiver and almost give out. A pair of strong hands wrapped around her, pulling her close.

"Easy now," Katrina heard him say, his face so close to hers she could feel his breath on her ear.

"Thank you," she whispered, feeling like she had been saying that a lot to him.

"Let's get you back in bed and in the morning, we can try walking again, and you can tell me more about why those men were trying to attack you."

Katrina didn't say anything, as he helped her back to the bed. She felt bad when he lay back on the floor beneath her. Her eyes closed, as her body felt tired from the short little walk. As she fell asleep, she tried to figure out what she was going to tell him tomorrow morning.

CHAPTER 5

Bryan awoke to the sound of Katrina's light breathing and Arthur making little noises from his bed. His furs were nice to sleep on when he was outside, but in his house, he preferred the feather bed he had made for himself. Standing up, stretching the tight muscles in his back, he walked over to the little one and gave him a smile, "So, what this morning? You decided to let us sleep in by not waking everyone up with your scream, huh?

When Arthur made a face, he chuckled picking him up, "Don't get all mad and start screaming now. It was nice of you to not wake everyone up with your cries."

Changing the cloth covering him first, Bryan kept up a steady chatter to keep the baby quiet before he fed him. Once the baby was changed, he sat on the chair feeding him from the bladder. He watched Arthur for a few minutes, as he hungrily sucked down his milk as if he hadn't been fed in days, not just a few hours.

"You act as if you haven't eaten in days, little one. It has not been that long, I promise you." Bryan knew that it was common for most babies to wake up several times throughout the night and was pleasantly surprised that Arthur woke up just once to feed.

A sound from the room caused Bryan to look up to see Katrina standing just outside the doorway, her hand on the wall as if she didn't quite trust herself to walk on her own. When he started to stand, she shook her head. "No. Take care of him, I'm okay."

Katrina took a few more steps keeping a hold on the wall. Bryan noticed a light sheen of sweat on her as she took a break, her breath coming in hard little pants. When Arthur was done eating, he laid him on the fur in the middle of the floor before walking to Katrina.

Katrina's eyes were half closed, her shoulders sagged. If Bryan had to guess, it was simply her stubborn will that kept her standing, more so than the wall she was leaning on. Before she could utter a protest, he bent down and picked her up in his arms, causing a small shriek to come from her. Bryan carried her the few steps to one of the chairs at the table and carefully placed her on it.

When he put her down, he noticed the blush on her cheeks. "Thank you."

Bryan smiled, her tone had a bit of a pout. "You've been in bed for days, and the only thing I've been able to get into you has been broth. It'll be a day or two before you're ready for solid foods. Your body is a little weak from fighting the fever and not having any sustenance."

He watched as she frowned at the information, all the while looking around. The wolves were still out, and he didn't really expect them back until later today. They were never gone too long, but most of the time when they went hunting he could expect them to be gone for at least two days.

His sister had told him that his house needed more color, saying it looked like a man lived here with no intention of taking a wife. Bryan had never considered taking a wife. Instead, he would visit a widow in his town who took care of his needs. He now found himself wondering what Katrina thought of his home. Was she comfortable here? Did she just see it as a man's home?

"Are you hungry?" Bryan asked after she seemed to come to whatever conclusion she had been mulling over.

"Yes, please," Katrina replied before giving her attention back to him. "I need to get back on my way to Camelot. His parents must be really anxious. Could I impose upon you to take me there or help me get a ride?" I will make sure you're paid for your troubles."

As he heated up the broth for her on the fire, he watched her out of the corner of his eye. Bryan knew she was not being honest about something. Had she kidnapped the baby for a ransom? Was she selling him to someone else? He couldn't come up with a reason why a newborn baby wouldn't be traveling with his mother, or with his wet nurse. Katrina was obviously none of these.

"You will need to regain most of your strength before you travel anywhere. In a few days, I can travel with you to town and put you on a carriage to Camelot," Bryan said as he made up her bowl.

She didn't say anything as he walked over to her with her food, she just watched the baby on the floor. She was exhausted from her small walk, and she was frustrated with his answers, but for him, it was interesting to watch her think about all possibilities.

After he fed her a few bites, she finally asked him the question he could see brewing. "When's the next time you expect a carriage to stop by. Maybe I could arrange something…"

Bryan shook his head, "It will be a long while. It's winter, and my home isn't near the main road. There are one or two that still come up here, but I don't know when."

Her shoulders slumped and when he went to feed her another

bite she shook her head. "You need to eat Katrina. Your body is hungry, even if you are too busy pouting to want anything."

"I'm not pouting," she said, glaring at him.

When he chuckled, and raised an eyebrow, she huffed and dutifully opened her mouth for the next bite. He got her to eat a little more before he caught her eyes trying to close. Putting down the spoon, he stood up and scooped her out of the chair to carry her back to the bed.

"You do not need to carry me," she said, as she looked up at him.

"True, but I fear you'll fall asleep before you get to my bed."

A blush spread on her cheeks, and he watched her face as she tried to look anywhere but at him. He bit his cheek to keep from smiling about her obvious discomfort, either at needing his help or the fact that she was sleeping in his bed. The rules of court were simple, and he knew that if she were caught in his bed, innocent or not, the rumors about that situation would ruin her.

Outside the confines of the castle, they were not as strict, but the fact that she was in his shirt and his bed would be damning, and she would be ruined. Bryan had seen her naked, and that was compromising no matter where they lived. "The baby will be taking another nap soon. Would you like me to put him in bed with you for a bit?"

"I would like that," she whispered, as he put her down. He tucked her in, propping up the pillow, so she could sit up while holding the baby.

When he got Arthur from the floor, he smiled. "You make sure you behave. I don't think she's up for one of your fits just yet."

The face Arthur gave him almost made him smile. If he didn't know any better, the little lad understood what he said and didn't appreciate it. When he walked into the room, he stopped to admire the beauty in his bed. Her brown hair had blond highlights. He liked it down and framing her face. He had an image of her in his bed, a soft blush on her cheeks, as she welcomed him with an inviting smile.

Arthur made a sound bringing him back to the present, causing him to shake his head. Having thoughts about a woman, who might have kidnapped the baby, in his arms was not the best thing for him to be lusting over.

"Here you go," he said, as he gently placed the baby into her open arms. She smiled down at the baby, her face relaxing.

Arthur gave Katrina one of his rare smiles that lit up his face. "You are good with babies. Do you have any?"

"No lass, I've never had one of my own. He's a good lad, who only fusses when he is wet or hungry. The milking bag was something I'd only seen used for animals before," Bryan said.

Katrina smiled down at the baby in her lap. "I've actually never seen one before, until they gave him to me and loaded us up in the carriage."

"Who loaded you into the carriage?" Bryan said leaning forward, curious if she was finally going to reveal more about herself.

Katrina opened her mouth before closing it again. After a moment of silence, she looked up at him. "Arthur's father put me in the carriage. Since my lady went into labor early the wet nurse wasn't traveling with us. We were lucky one of the groomsmen had used something similar and had modified it for the baby."

Bryan nodded. She was lying to him. He wasn't sure why, but as long as she was, he would need to be careful. "I'll check on you both in a little bit."

Katrina let out a slow breath, as he walked out of the room. She knew she'd almost slipped and said something she shouldn't. She had to keep him safe. Katrina smiled down at the baby. When they put him in her arms the first time, she could barely stand the idea of holding him. But when she was running from those men in the woods, she would have given her life to save him.

She should fear Bryan. He was a giant of a man, and she was defenseless against him. But he had taken care of her, and Arthur. He hadn't pushed, even though Katrina was positive he knew she was lying to him. She was a horrible liar. The Queen had often said she brought her with her, because she needed one person who would tell her the truth. "Your mother used to like laughing at me when I was a kid. Said we could never get away with anything, because everyone knew when I was lying."

Arthur watched her intently, and she felt guilty for her thoughts on the ride to Merlin's. "I made a promise to keep you safe and I will. Your parents must be really worried about you."

The Queen was her friend, and she had been so excited when she told her she thought she was pregnant. It was a hard pregnancy, made harder by Morgana who had been the only dark spot in her friend's life. Katrina sent up a small prayer to the gods that she would get Arthur to his mother soon.

Arthur yawned, blinking his eyes slowly, and she smiled as she laid the baby next to her, mimicking his yawn with one of her own. As she closed her eyes, she put her hand on his belly hoping soon she could go home.

CHAPTER 6

Katrina woke the next afternoon to see a big wolf standing over the baby. She covered her mouth to keep from screaming, as she tried to figure out how to move the big animal. Where was Bryan? Was he dead?

The wolf turned toward her, its golden-brown eyes peering at her curiously. As she frantically searched around the room, she noticed the small fire that Bryan kept in the room was still lit. Maybe she could use that to get the wolf away from the bed. As she eased herself to the bottom of the bed, she rallied all her strength to stand up and tried to figure out how she could use the fire to scare the wolf off.

As she stumbled off the bed, she let out a small squeak, and the wolf took a step toward her. Katrina looked around trying to figure out what she could grab to scare the wolf away, when she saw Bryan appear in the doorway. A sigh of relief escaped her, and she whispered his name trying to get his attention.

Bryan turned, and the grin on his face faded when he saw her. When he rushed to her, she put her hands up. "The wolf! We need to get it away from Arthur."

Bryan frowned, confused, before finally saying, "Minx, out!" while pointing to the door.

When the wolf huffed, Katrina felt a moment of panic thinking Bryan might be delusional. When he simply pointed to the door and said *out* again, she blinked watching the wolf walk out the door without incident.

Before she could ask one of the many questions rolling around in her head, Bryan was next to her, his arm coming out to help her stand. "Are you okay? Did you hurt yourself getting out of bed?"

"There was a wolf standing over the baby--" Katrina started to say, when she realized that the wolf had listened to him. She took a step back causing him to let go of her. "The wolf, it listened to you."

Was he a warlock like Merlin, or maybe he was a demon working with those men who had attacked her? "I've raised that wolf's mate since he was a pup. When the two mated, she moved in. Minx's' pup died last year, and she seems to really love watching Arthur."

"You let a wolf near him?" Katrina practically shrieked the words.

Arthur let out a cry after her shriek, and she realized she must have either awakened him or startled him. As she took a step forward, she felt Bryan's arms slip around her pulling her close. He wasn't wearing a shirt, again, and her hand had nowhere to go but his chest. His skin felt warm under her hand. He wasn't hairy but instead had a light trail of hair that disappeared into his pants.

"I would never let anyone hurt you or the babe," Bryan said against her ear.

Katrina tilted her head to look up at him. His face was so close, she could feel his breath on her lips. She knew she should fight against him, but at this moment, she couldn't remember why. Her breath caught in her throat, and she started to wonder what it would feel like if he kissed her.

The sound of Arthur whimpering snapped her out of her thoughts, and when she pushed gently, he released her easily. Her legs steadier than they were earlier, she made it to Arthur's bed. She bent down to pick him up, holding him to her as he fussed.

She looked over at Bryan who was watching her. "You have two wolves?"

"I have four," he said calmly, as he kept an eye on her. "Do you remember the day you were attacked by those men in the woods?"

"Yes," she said, nodding as she went and sat on the edge of her bed.

"Do you remember how you got away from those men?" She frowned thinking about it. The man was holding her, and she was trying to think of how to get away. She remembered hearing a growl, and a flash of white before he let her go. It had been a wolf that saved her.

"He was attacked by a white wolf," Katrina said. "I didn't see much after that, just white fur and then I ran."

Bryan nodded, taking a step toward her, putting his hand on her elbows as she held the baby to her. "Snow saved you and then followed you into the woods and lay against you. He was the reason the two of you didn't freeze to death. With the snow falling, I might not have been able to find you after you ran away."

Katrina sort of remembered a white figure coming toward her. She didn't think it was a person, but she was so tired and cold by then she couldn't be sure. But, the wolf that was just in here was a darker wolf. "You have four wolves. One of which you claim saved me."

She felt Bryan reach up, push a piece of hair and place it behind her ear. "I would say I did it all by myself, but there were a lot of men after you, and I would never have been able to save you on my own."

For some reason, that confession made her smile. She didn't realize how close he had moved as he spoke until she realized the only thing between the two of them was the baby. Her mouth suddenly dry, she licked her lips as her eyes met his. A blush spread on her cheeks when she realized he was watching her mouth. "Are you sure they will not harm us?"

Bryan smiled down at her. "Are you brave enough to let me show you?"

Her spine straightened, and she nodded. "Let me put Arthur down."

Before she could move, Bryan took him from her arms. When he smiled down at the baby in his arms, she felt her heart skip a small beat. "Can you stay in your bed while I introduce Katrina to your friend Minx?"

It almost looked like Arthur smiled back at him, which was silly. He was too young to smile at him let alone understand what he had said. She watched him place the baby gently in the crib before stepping closer to her. When he stood before her, she gathered her courage. For some reason, him finding her weak upset her.

CHAPTER 7

Bryan watched the emotion on her face. It was like she was battling something internally. Once she agreed, he offered her his arm, and together they walked into the living room. Snow and Minx were both lying by the fireplace. The other two were in the barn.

Snow stood up, and he felt Katrina stiffen next to him. Minx yawned, appearing bored, but he noticed how she kept an eye on them. Except for his family, the wolves had always made themselves scarce around people. He hardly ever had a guest that stayed more than a day, but the circumstances that had brought Katrina were not normal.

"Snow," he said, calling the wolf to him.

Katrina moved in behind him as the wolf came closer. He couldn't blame her for being scared. Snow was big for a wolf. If he stood on his back legs, Snow dwarfed him. When Snow stood before him, he looked at Katrina curiously.

A hand up in the air Bryan said, "Sit."

Snow gave him a look that let him know he didn't appreciate being talked to like a common dog. After a long moment, Snow decided to humor him and sat down. Bryan looked over his shoulder at the woman who was half hiding behind him. "I promise Snow won't hurt you. Would you like to pet him?"

"Pet him?" she barely squeaked out the question, and he laughed.

"Yes. Pet him," Bryan said, as he reached out and petted the wolf to show her it would be all right.

He could feel Katrina stiffen next to him, as she pulled herself to her full height and took a step to stand next to him. Snow must have sensed what he was doing because he put his head down in a rare submissive position and patiently waited.

Bryan watched as Katrina finally reached out and touched Snow on the top of the head. He saw her smile when Snow bumped her hand encouraging her to continue. When she finally spoke, he heard the awe in her voice. "Thank you, for saving me Snow."

Snow bumped her hand, and when he stood up, Katrina pulled her hand back, a small gasp escaping her. Snow walked around her rubbing himself on her, and marking her with his scent before he bumped her hand again with his nose and licked her.

Snow had marked her as part of his pack. Katrina might not have understood the symbolism of what he'd just done, but Bryan did. Bryan trusted Snow's instincts better than his own and decided if Snow trusted Katrina, he could too.

That didn't mean he was going to stop asking her questions. "Minx over there is Snow's mate. There are two more that are in the barn. When I rescued Snow as a pup, his brother was with him. The two never left, even after Snow was well enough to do so."

Katrina looked up at him and gave him a smile. "So, you're often out saving those in need."

He blushed at her words of praise. When her smile grew, he shook his head, rubbing the back of his neck. "I did what anyone else would do," he said with a shrug of his shoulder, feeling uncomfortable.

She shook her head. "No, not everyone."

Bryan cleared his throat. He heard a sound form Arthur in the back room, and he gave her a nod before walking back to him. "He'll be wanting to eat now."

Bryan went and picked up Arthur. "You're about to complain that we are taking too long to feed you, huh, little laddie?"

Arthur let out a sound of complaint that made him laugh. Bryan turned to see Katrina watching. Her face had softened again, and that look on her face made his chest swell with male pride. Bryan could get used to that look.

"Would you like to feed him in bed?" he asked her, as she continued to watch.

Katrina wrinkled her nose, and Bryan couldn't help but grin. He had an image of her as a child making that face when her mother or father tried to get her to sit still. "Would it be all right if I fed him in the front room?"

Bryan nodded and offered her the baby when he got to her in the doorway. Once Arthur was settled in her arms, he put her hand on his back and walked her to the living room in case her legs decided she had been up long enough.

Once Katrina was settled in the chair, Bryan took care of getting her the milk and even brought a new changing cloth from the one's he had cleaned. Hopefully, soon the snow would stop, and the merchant would stop by, otherwise, he would need to start cutting up one of his old shirts or blankets.

The snow lasted for a few more days, and Bryan felt his feelings for Katrina grow. Since Katrina had only the one dress, she had started wearing his shirts while washing it. She was adorable, but he knew that she was embarrassed about not having something more appropriate to wear.

The wolves left a few days ago for a hunt, and after the fifth day Bryan felt himself worrying. They very rarely left for longer than three days at a time, so when the morning of the fifth day started, he found himself watching outside for them.

Katrina walked up behind him. When she touched his arm, he smiled down at her. "You're worried about them?"

Bryan thought about lying but instead nodded. "They don't usually leave for this long. I'm just hoping that they're playing in the snow."

She stood close to him. With Arthur down for his afternoon nap, she had decided to take a bath and had left her hair down. He fought the urge to reach out and run his fingers through it. The light from the window shone off the blond highlights. The more time they spent together, the harder it was for him to keep himself at a distance. Even though she never spoke about her life, he knew she was a highborn lady and not meant for someone like him.

She stood with him at the window, when they heard a carriage coming up the road. "Looks like the merchant was finally able to make it."

Katrina smiled, her face lighting up. He chuckled as he watched her. "Hopefully he has some cloth or a dress for you and some things for Arthur."

The smile on Katrina's face showed her happiness and excitement over the idea of a new dress. Together, they watched the carriage roll up to the house. When the merchant stopped in front of the home, Bryan opened the door to greet him.

The old man's face lit up when he saw Katrina step out. "Have you finally taken a wife Bryan?"

Bryan shook his head, rubbing the back of his neck, trying to think of what to say in order to keep Katrina's reputation intact.

Before he could reply, Katrina spoke up, "Bryan here was kind enough to give me shelter during the storm."

The merchant nodded. "It was a bad storm, lass. It was good of him to keep you safe. Plus, there have been lots of attacks on the roads."

"Do you have any material or dresses that she could use while she's stuck here? There's also an infant who needs some clothes as well," Bryan said as Katrina walked closer to the carriage.

"I believe I have just what she's looking for." The merchant opened the back of his carriage and revealed a chest. Bryan watched as he pulled out several different pieces of material and a couple of dresses he had and laid them out before Katrina. "These dresses might be a little big, but with a little adjustment they should fit beautifully."

As Katrina looked them over, the merchant talked with Bryan, "Have you heard about the attacks on the kingdom? They say Morgana might have killed the King and is now searching for the prince."

Bryan noticed how Katrina froze when the merchant mentioned Morgana. "Are they sure that the King is dead? What about the Queen?"

The merchant nodded. "They said he was attacked on the way back to the castle after visiting Merlin. The castle has been raided, the Queen is missing, and Morgana is furious that the prince is nowhere to be found. She is searching for all newborn boy babies."

Katrina had gone still her head tilted toward them. Bryan watched her out of the corner of his eye. "Have you seen anything on the roads?"

"There have been men roaming, looking for something. So far, I've been lucky. I've seen people with tattoos on their faces; they left me alone." The merchant frowned as he glanced at Katrina. "You better be careful with that baby. Those men are close."

Before Katrina could reply, Bryan spoke up, "Katrina has a little girl. We will keep her safe from those men. Who is acting as king now?" Brian asked hoping to distract him.

"The King's brother has taken over. He says he will find the prince first and raise him to be king," said the merchant.

Bryan asked a few more questions while Katrina picked out two dresses, material, and some cloth for the baby. While Bryan paid the merchant, Katrina went into the house. After the merchant left, Bryan debated about asking Katrina about Arthur. Is he the prince Morgana was looking for? Had Katrina saved him, or had she kidnapped him? What was he going to do?

When he opened the door, he saw Katrina standing in the middle of the front room. Her hands were clenched in front of herself, as she chewed her bottom lip. Bryan still had not decided what to do. Instead, he picked up the blue material saying, "This will make a nice shirt for Arthur."

Katrina nodded, "Thank you. As soon as I get home, I'll pay you back."

Bryan noticed the small catch in her voice when she said home. He gave her a nod, not overly concerned with her paying him back. He was more concerned with the idea that Arthur might be the prince. And if he was indeed the prince, how did he end up with Katrina? Was she his savior or kidnapper?

He knew the men with tattoos on their faces were the men that had been attacking Katrina. If Morgana's men were attacking her, had she double-crossed them?

"The men that he said were on the roads, the one's with the tattoos, do you think they were the one's attacking you and Arthur?" Bryan asked watching her intently.

Katrina dropped the cloth she was holding. He noticed how she refused to pick up her head and bit her lip as she bent down to retrieve it. Katrina stood back up and put the cloth on the table before finally answering him. "I, umm, didn't know who those men were, or why they attacked us. One minute everything was fine, and suddenly those men were surrounding us."

She was a horrible liar. She still refused to meet his eyes. Instead she ran her fingers along the material. Bryan needed to know. "Katrina, did you kidnap the prince? Were you working with Morgana and changed your mind when you were supposed to turn him over?"

Katrina's head snapped up, her hand going to her chest when he noticed the hurt look on her face. "You think I would work with that woman to kidnap that baby?"

Bryan watched her. "I know he's not your son, Katrina. You've been keeping secrets. I will protect you if you need it, but I need to know from what."

He watched as she fidgeted. Her fingers were playing with the material as she nervously chewed on her lower lip. Bryan watched as several emotions crossed her face, until finally, she let out a deep breath, her shoulders sagging in defeat.

"I'm one of the Queen's companions. I came with her when she was brought over to marry the King. We grew up together. When Arthur was born, they put him in my arms and told me to take him to Merlin's. The King was there with him, waiting. Merlin said he had to help prepare him for what was to come. The King and Merlin told me it was my job to protect Arthur. The King left before we did, and we were attacked on our way back to the castle," Katrina told him, finally meeting his gaze.

Bryan, was silent, feeling his world getting smaller. He didn't regret saving her and the baby, but what danger did that put him in? Morgana was ruthless. If she found out that he was hiding the prince, she would attack him without mercy. Is that why his wolves hadn't come home yet? As he debated about what to do, he watched Katrina study him.

Before he could wrap his mind around what he had just learned, Arthur started crying. Katrina excused herself and left Bryan alone with his thoughts. His head swam, and he took deep breaths, determined to tell her that she should go back home. When he got to the doorway, he stopped in his tracks. The light from the window was shining on them, she held the baby close to her chest, her eyes closed as she whispered, "It's okay my little prince, I'll keep you safe. There's no need to cry."

The realization that this small woman would be willing to sacrifice herself for this helpless baby meant he couldn't tell her to leave. "Here, let me try and soothe him," he said, moving closer.

Katrina met him in the middle of the room, and he could tell by her shaky hands, that she was nervous about what he would do with this new information. Bryan took Arthur into his arms and gently rocked the little guy. As he looked down, he saw Arthur's green eyes full of tears and his bottom lip quivering.

Bryan held Arthur to his chest making little *shh* noises as he bounced him gently in his arms; something he had learned to do while Katrina was still unconscious. It didn't take long for Arthur to calm down. Once he was settled, Bryan motioned for Katrina to follow him out of the room. While settling Arthur on the fur bed on the floor, he could see Katrina pacing the front room.

"With the castle under attack and the King dead you can't take Arthur back there," Bryan pointed out wondering what she was thinking.

"I don't know what to do. I should take him back to his mother... she must be worried. What if she's hiding and waiting for me to bring back her son."

Bryan walked toward her, put his hands on her arms and held her still. He waited for her to look at him. She was scared. He could see it in her eyes, so he reached up and brushed the hair back from her face. "Katrina, we have to keep you both safe. Even if she is safe and hiding, your job is to protect yourself and Arthur."

CHAPTER 8

Katrina slowly nodded, understanding the truth in his words. When she nodded in agreement, she expected Bryan to pull away. Instead, she felt his hands caressing her arms in a way she was sure was meant to be reassuring, but instead caused her to shudder with a need to be closer to him.

"I don't want to put you in danger," Katrina whispered, realizing that in the short time they'd been together, she had already started to care for him.

Bryan smiled at her and dipped his head to brush his lips against hers, causing her to gasp in surprise. His eyes twinkled, and he did it again. This time, she felt his lips curve in a smile. "Let Morgana try to take you and the lad from me."

Despite being scared, she couldn't help but smile at him. Tempted to give in to the urge to kiss him, she leaned forward, only to stop when Arthur started making noises on the blanket. Before she could walk away, Bryan kissed her one time, quick and hard, before releasing her.

Without a word, he walked out the front door, leaving her alone with Arthur and her thoughts. Katrina felt her cheeks heat up and knew she was blushing as she walked over to Arthur and sat with him on the floor. When he smiled, laughing up at her, she giggled, feeling younger than she had in years.

"I think we'll be okay," she said, as she picked Arthur up to put him on her lap.

He had grown so much. He was already trying to hold his head up, and she bet that, soon, he would be rolling over. "You know your mother loves you so much. She was so excited when she told me she was expecting you. She knew you were going to be a boy."

Arthur gurgled up at her, and she smiled. She felt a wave of sadness thinking about her friend. Yes, she was her Queen, but before that, they were friends. Just two little girls who played tag outside and would often sneak out and hide from their tutor together. They often talked about their dreams, about one day being married and having children.

Becoming a Queen's companion had put her dreams of being a wife and mother on hold. She didn't regret her choice, but now she had nowhere to go. Could she stay here with Bryan? Did he want her to? If not, could he help her get home to her family with the baby?

There were so many unanswered questions. After a few minutes of playing with Arthur on the floor, she heard the door open and looked up to see Bryan. "I'm starting to worry about the wolves. I am going to go out for a bit and see if I can find them in one of their usual hunting spots. There are a few that are close to the house."

Katrina nodded, biting her lip, and watched as he walked over to her. He bent down and patted Arthur on the head, then surprised her by brushing his finger across her cheek. "Stay inside while I am gone. I won't be long, I promise."

She nodded. This wasn't the first time he had left her alone. Normally, one of the wolves stayed with her. Since she had been awake, this was the longest they had been gone. Arthur loved the wolves, and despite her misgivings, they seemed to be gentle with him. She had often found the female lying on the floor with him. Snow, the alpha of the pack from what she could tell, never got near Arthur but instead was often watching from afar.

As the day dragged on Katrina did her best to clean up the house. She wasn't used to cleaning, and her hands hurt from the scrubbing. She never thought of herself as spoiled or even thought about what the housemaids must go through. Her back ached after scrubbing the floor. She didn't even get done with more than half of it before she stopped to sit on the chair. As Katrina stretched her back, she looked out the window and realized how far the sun had gone down.

Katrina did know how to cook a few things, so she put together what she needed for the stew. As she hummed to herself, she tried to think about anything other than the fact that Bryan had been gone for so long. Once that was done, she heard Arthur begin to fuss and knew it was about time for him to be changed and fed.

After taking care of Arthur, she checked the food. It had been a long time since she had cooked, and she felt proud of herself that it smelled edible. After lighting a few more candles, she spread the new fabric out on the floor next to Arthur. "You're growing too big. We need to make you something new to wear."

Arthur smiled and grabbed at his feet. Katrina couldn't help but grin as she watched him. Bryan had bought her everything she would need, including thread and needles. She used the pins to mark the fabric and went to work.

Katrina lost herself in creating an outfit and chatting with him and occasionally making sure to get up to stir the stew. When her stomach started to rumble, she found herself debating if she should just go ahead and eat.

Before she could make up her mind, the door flew open, and in walked Bryan. She smiled, jumping up from the floor to go to him. Katrina threw her arms around his neck holding him tight, blushing when she heard his soft grunt.

She started to pull away after she realized what she had done and felt him wrap his arms around her. She gave in to the urge to hold him a few minutes longer before stepping back. Her cheeks felt hot, and she knew she was blushing.

"Did you find them?" she asked, knowing when he left he was really worried about his wolves.

Bryan shook his head. "I saw hints of them but didn't actually find them," Bryan said, pausing. She watched as his hand came up and pushed a piece of stray hair back behind her ear.

"Sorry I worried you lass. I didn't mean to be gone so long."

Katrina nodded grasping her hands in front of herself before rocking on her heels. "I've made stew for when you returned."

"You made supper?" Bryan asked.

Katrina smiled at the note of surprise in his voice. She nodded, "It's one of the few things I know how to make. My mother decided that I should know something for those times when we were traveling."

Bryan, she noticed, looked with interest toward the pot that was hanging over the fire. "I need to clean up and will tell you what I saw as we enjoy your delicious meal."

His simple words of praise made her smile. She watched Bryan go over and greet Arthur who smiled and cooed at the big man pouting a bit when he left. Katrina took the time to make two bowls of stew. Bryan had baked bread two days ago and she placed it on the wooden table along with two cups of cider.

Once Arthur was settled closer to the table, she saw Bryan come out of the room. Both sat at the table. She watched him as he tentatively took his first bite. She hid a smile as she noticed how he hesitated first. His eyes widened, and she watched as he nodded. "This is good."

Katrina beamed, feeling a sense of pride at something so silly. Women cooked for men all the time. She hadn't, but others did. Katrina took a bite of her own food and was happy to taste that it had turned out well and wasn't only edible but rather good if she did say so herself.

"You said you saw hints of them?" Katrina asked after they both took a few more bites of their food.

"There's a trail several miles from here. It looks like they are tracking a group of men."

She frowned. "Do they normally track men?"

Bryan shook his head. "No. But I've never seen a group this big before. The only other time they have ever tracked men was when they were…"

Bryan's voice trailed off and she nodded realizing that he was talking about the time they had saved her. "Do you think they're tracking Morgana's men?"

After a long pause, he nodded. He watched her as he took another bite. Katrina thought about what he'd just said. Not only was her home under attack, but her Queen was missing. Her family was so far away, she realized she was now completely on her own. When Arthur made a noise demanding her attention she bent down to pick him up thinking she also had a baby to keep safe while Morgana's men hunted him.

Lost in thought she jumped when she felt Bryan take her hand and squeeze it gently. "Lass, I see your mind spinning. I promise to keep you both safe."

She nodded and realized, somehow, he would. Bryan was strong enough for her to lean on. She gave him a smile and heard Arthur gurgle his happy noise. The two of them finished eating and Katrina couldn't help but give him the occasional glance out of the corner of her eye.

When they'd both finished eating Katrina got up to lay Arthur down so she could clean up the pot she'd used when Bryan stopped her. "I'll take care of that while you put him to bed."

There was something in the way he looked at her that made her shudder. She nodded, her body responding to the hungry way he watched her. Taking care of Arthur, she sat on the bed and rocked him gently, humming softly. When Arthur finally fell asleep in her arms, she got up and gently put him in his bed covering him with the fur.

Katrina quietly walked to the front room and saw Bryan staring out the window as he sat on the chair. She smiled, his concern for the wolves made him even more endearing. She stepped up behind him and put her hand on his shoulder. "I'm sure they are fine."

He nuzzled her hand with his cheek before Skissing it gently. When his eyes met hers, she whispered, "I was scared something might have happened to you while you were out."

Bryan didn't say anything, instead he grabbed her hand and moved to pull her onto his lap. When he looked deep into her eyes, she felt vulnerable. "There was no way I wasn't coming home to you and Arthur."

Those words on his tongue gave her hope. Her lips parted, and she wanted to ask him what he meant when he interrupted her thoughts with a kiss. His tongue slid into her mouth, and she let out a small moan. Her fingers found their way into his hair, and she held him tight, as her world seemed to spin with his kiss. Bryan pulled back and gently put his forehead against hers. She was happy to see he was breathing just as hard as she.

"Katrina, if you want me to stop, please tell me now," Bryan said and she opened her eyes to look right at him.

He was giving her the option. There were so many reasons to say no. But, as she sat on his lap, and he waited patiently for her answer, she couldn't find a reason that would matter.

CHAPTER 9

Bryan waited for her to reply. He could see the surprise on her face when he asked her if she wanted to stop. Katrina was a beautiful woman who deserved better than him. As the Queen's lady, she had spent her days surrounded by men who could provide her with a home and servants. Bryan could give her a home, he would protect her and Arthur with his life, but she could have so much more.

When Katrina slid from his lap, he put his head down and realized she had chosen to stop. The wave of disappointment that hit him would have knocked him off his feet if he were standing. When he felt her hand slide into his and tug gently, he looked up at her and saw a faint blush on her cheeks as she smiled down at him.

"Are you sure, lass?" Bryan asked, almost afraid of what she would say.

Katrina nodded, biting her lip, and he stood up then bent down to carry her to the bedroom. He knew that they would have to be quiet since Arthur was sleeping in the room, but he didn't care. He had thought about her naked and under him almost every night since she had awakened from her fever. When he put her down, he reached up to undo the laces in the front of her gown before stepping behind her to undo the string back there.

With her dress loosened, he watched as she shrugged letting the dress fall from her body and pool around her feet. He noticed how she stiffened a bit and he smiled while kissing her shoulder. "You are beautiful."

Katrina glanced over her shoulder at him, the gold in her brown eyes reflecting the light from the fire. Bryan turned her in his arms, brushing his lips back and forth across hers. When he felt her relax, he tried to give her a reassuring smile. Even though she responded to his kiss, he could tell she had little to no experience, and he wanted to make sure that even though there would be some discomfort the first time, she would still find pleasure.

"If you ever want to stop--" he started to say when she silenced him with a kiss.

Katrina wrapped her arms around him and a moan escaped when he felt her tongue come out and touch his lips. She was taking control and Bryan loved her boldness mixed with innocence. Her tongue tentatively entered his mouth and slid across his tongue causing him to tighten his hold on her. His tongue dueled with hers and he let her set the pace, pushing when she thrust. When she broke the kiss, he moaned and she smiled, a pretty blush staining her cheeks.

"I trust you, always," she whispered against his lips.

With that she took a step back, and he watched as she slowly removed the rest of her clothes. He noticed how Katrina kept her eyes averted and never looked at him and as soon as she was naked she quickly slid into the bed, pulling the blankets up to cover herself.

One day, hopefully soon, he wished to enjoy the sight of her naked body by the firelight, but right now he would just take advantage of being able to touch her. While kicking off his leather boots, he pulled his shirt up and over his head and tossed it to the side then reached up to undo the tie on his pants.

Not wanting to embarrass her, he quickly removed his pants, but before he could get into bed, he happened to see Katrina staring at his groin with a look of curiosity. He could feel himself getting harder under her widened gaze, and she released a small gasp of surprise while her cheeks reddened even more.

Bryan got in bed. Going under the covers, he bit his lip to keep from smiling. He noticed how her eyes had widened and her muscles tensed. She reminded him of a frightened deer about to dash. Brushing her hair back from her face, he leaned over and kissed her. He kept it light, waiting for her to relax before deepening it. When he heard her soft moan, and felt her lips part under his, he deepened the kiss. When she moved closer to him, he felt he'd won a small victory.

Once she was totally relaxed against him, he pushed her onto her back. Bryan slid his hand from her shoulder to cup her breast, brushing his thumb back and forth against the sensitive nub, which hardened against his touch. When she arched her back, he released her lips and bent his head to suck on her nipple.

Katrina cried out and he felt her hands slide into his hair. Despite the fact that he could feel her body still tense under him, she responded to his touch with a passion that made him want to please her more.

Bryan teased each of her breasts until her body was squirming under his. He pulled back to look down at her. Katrina's face was flushed, her eyes closed, and her lips swelled from his kisses. "Beautiful," he whispered.

When she opened her eyes and met his, he saw that they had darkened with desire. Bryan tentatively rocked his hips, his cock sliding between her folds, teasing her as he rubbed on her. "Bryan," she whispered, as her hips moved against him.

He bent down and nuzzled her cheek as he continued to rock

against her enjoying the sensations when she moved back against him. "Do you want me to stop, lass?"

Her breath came out in small pants and she shook her head while whispering, "No. Don't stop."

Taking it slow was killing him, but he knew if he rushed it tonight, he would hurt her. Katrina trusted him, and he was determined to make sure she enjoyed her first time. Bryan slid one hand from her breast, down the rounded curve of her stomach, past the dark curls that covered all her secrets and slid his finger between her folds.

Bryan felt Katrina's thighs tighten at first touch. "Relax for me. Open for me," he whispered against her neck.

She nodded and he grinned and felt her tighten more when he brushed the hard nub at the top of her core. Up and down, he stroked slowly, deepening the pressure until he felt Katrina's muscles relax and her legs part giving him better access to all of her bodily secrets.

Bryan claimed her mouth with a kiss, thrusting his tongue as he pushed his finger into her. His mouth swallowed her soft cry and he felt her pull back, her legs tightening on his hips. He waited for her to adjust to the intrusion, before he began to move his finger slowly in and out of her, mimicking the action of his tongue as he kissed her.

When Katrina started to move her hips, he slowly inserted a second finger. Stretching her and getting her ready for his body, as he kissed her. His cock was painfully hard, and he wanted nothing more than to bury himself deep inside her.

Breaking the kiss, he looked down at her, and when he withdrew his fingers from her core, he couldn't help but feel the swell of male pride as she whimpered in protest. Bryan positioned the head of his cock at her entrance. When she blinked open her eyes, he brushed the hair from her face. "Bryan…" she whispered his name curiously as if wondering why he waited.

"I'm sorry," he said, as he pushed into her. Her body was so tight, and it felt like her muscles were contracting around him in protest. When he felt the barrier of her innocence give, he heard her cry of pain and felt her nails dig into his back.

Once he was deep inside her, he held still, waiting for her to adjust to his size. He could feel beads of sweat forming along his body, as his muscles began to shake. When he felt her move slightly under him causing him to slide deeper into her, he groaned wondering if it was possible to die from holding back.

∽

Katrina moved under him again, but this time she didn't feel the same searing pain as before but instead felt a stirring. She moved again and felt a pleasurable sensation that caused her to moan in pleasure.

Katrina looked up at Bryan and noticed the fine shine of sweat and the way his jaw was set so tight. She moved again, his growl vibrating along her chest as he watched her. "Are you okay?" he asked between gritted teeth.

She nodded, moving again. "Bryan, is there more?" she asked feeling oddly unsatisfied and wishing they could go back to the kissing part.

Bryan smiled down at her and he pulled out before pushing back in. This time the feeling was pleasant and that sensation she felt earlier started to stir. "So much more, lass."

With that, he kissed her again as his hips kept a slow pace of pulling out before thrusting back in. Katrina moaned as her pleasure began to build again. His movement started slow, and she found herself wanting more. Unable to catch her breath she broke the kiss holding on to his shoulders. "Bryan," she panted.

His hand slid from her hip to her breast where he gently cupped it, teasing it with his fingers pinching it, rolling it between his fingers causing a stirring sensation from her breast to her core. Each tug, each flick, causing her pleasure to build.

When she felt her world stop, the pleasure rising to the point of almost being painful, she heard Bryan whisper in her ear, "Let go, Katrina, I've got you."

Katrina didn't understand what he meant, but the next thing she knew a wave of pleasure seemed to explode, and she screamed into the crook of his neck. The sound muffled so she wouldn't wake the baby. Wave after delicious wave rolled through her. When she heard his grunt and felt his hard thrust inside her, she wondered if he felt as good as she did. She also wondered why no one had ever told her that it would be so pleasurable.

When they both finally caught their breath, she felt Bryan shift and whimper as he slipped from her. She cupped his cheek and he looked down at her and said, "Did I hurt you?"

He raised an eyebrow when she said no, so she shook her head and admitted, "Only for a moment."

Katrina reached up and pushed his hair back behind his shoulder. She was touched by his obvious concern. "I promise I'm okay."

Bryan nodded, giving her a gentle kiss before moving off the bed. She missed his heat when he left and watched as he grabbed a cloth, wetting it with water that was in the basin. She watched as he approached the bed.

Katrina felt her cheeks heat up when she realized what he was planning. As he moved the furs away from her, he began to gently clean between her thighs. He cleaned himself up before joining her back in the bed.

Bryan reached out and put an arm around her, pulling her close and forcing her to lie on his chest. Katrina kept her head down, sighing when she felt his thumb brush back and forth across her cheek. She looked up at him and felt her heart do a small jump at the way he looked at her.

"You and Arthur are going to stay with me," Bryan finally said, breaking the silence.

Katrina was stunned by his words. She had thought about going back to her home country but knew she would probably never make it to the port with all of Morgana's men out there. Bryan raised an eyebrow and she realized he was still waiting for her to agree.

"We will put you in danger," Katrina said, feeling guilty because she knew if he pushed she would stay.

Bryan made a snort giving her a look that said he was obviously not scared, "You'll stay. I'll keep you both safe."

His tone was firm, and she blushed, nodding. "We'll stay with you."

Bryan nodded, and he reached, up sliding his finger along her jaw whispering, "You should sleep now."

Katrina giggled as she put her head down on his chest. When she closed her eyes, she found all the excitement and events from the day catching up to her. The sound of his strong heartbeat and the feel of his hand stroking up and down her back, lulled her into a deep sleep.

As she stretched awake, Katrina felt a tightening between her thighs reminding her of the night before. She opened her eyes, surprised to find the bed empty next to her. The amount of light coming in from the window let her know she had slept in later than usual. Surprised that Arthur had let her sleep in, she got up from the bed to check on him.

Not finding Arthur in his bed she listened, smiling when she heard Arthur making cooing noises from the living room. Getting dressed quickly, she used the brush on Bryan's chest. Katrina left her hair down, using a leather strand to tie it back.

Before she stepped from the room, she blushed thinking about what they'd done last night. She had given herself to him. Afterwards, he had told her he wanted her to stay with them.

Bryan never mentioned love or wanting to marry her. Maybe he meant to keep her as his mistress.

The idea that he wanted her just as a mistress made her a bit sad. The dye had already been cast he had already taken her body and Katrina realized that she was falling in love with him. Bryan not only rescued her but was also kind enough to take care of a newborn baby and nurse her back to health. Not to mention that he had rescued and raised wolves. She had no idea what the future held, but she knew Bryan would take care of her. She had trusted him with her body.

She stepped from the room and walked into the living room, smiling when she found Bryan sitting in the chair holding Arthur to his chest, feeding him from the bladder. With Bryan so big the baby looked tiny in his arms. Where Katrina grew up, men very rarely took the time to hold their babies, so watching Bryan do it with such ease had often surprised her.

When Bryan caught her watching him, she smiled, her cheeks heating up and she knew she was blushing. He gave her a wink that made her heart flutter in her chest before he spoke up. "I thought I would let you sleep this morning and take care of him."

Katrina took the few steps to him and saw Arthur eating happily in his arms. Arthur must have sensed her watching him. Katrina knew she was doing what her friend would want, keeping her son safe. But she couldn't help but feel guilty when she realized her friend might be dead and might never be able to see her son, watch him grow, or hear him call her mama.

She didn't even realize she had shed a tear for her friend until she heard Bryan say, "Are you thinking about his family?"

Katrina nodded, reaching down and tracing his cheek with her finger. "I grew up with the Queen. We were best friends and now I don't even know if she's alive or not. The King's thought to be dead and I have her son, who's being hunted by both Morgana and his uncle. Both will have him killed the moment they find him."

She watched as Bryan looked down at Arthur, "Well lass, we'll just have to make sure they never find him. We'll keep him safe."

She believed him. He would keep Arthur safe and protect her from whatever came their way. On impulse, she bent down and brushed her lips against his. When she stood up straight, she noticed how his eyes had darkened with desire causing a small shudder to run down her spine.

CHAPTER 10

After a few days, the wolves finally came home. Bryan was feeding the horses when Snow walked into the barn and dropped a hand at his feet. Bryan picked it up and noticed the marking. It was similar to the facial tattoos on the men that had been hunting Katrina and Arthur. Snow and the other wolves must have run into a group of them and killed at least one of them. When Bryan crawled in bed with Katrina that night, he debated about telling her. When she curled up in his arms and tilted her face up for a kiss he pushed it from his mind and gave in to the need to make love to her.

Katrina responded to his every touch and mirrored them with one of her own. He loved the way she seemed to get bolder each time. Bryan loved her curious nature and she learned quickly what pleased him. Katrina seemed to enjoy pushing him to the point where he couldn't hold back anymore, and he would take her. They both tried to be quiet for the baby sleeping in the room and she often either buried her head in his neck to muffle her scream or just bit him hard on his shoulder. Bryan had never let a woman bite him before and he found himself deeply enjoying it.

Bryan smiled, his chest puffing up with pride at her flushed cheeks and smile playing on her lips in the aftermath of taking her. "I would like to take you to visit my sister soon. You can stay there while I build us a bigger home."

Katrina's eyes lit up when she mentioned staying with his sister. But her shoulders sagged and she bit her lower lip before she asked quietly. "What will your sister think about... us?"

Not understanding her question at first, he frowned. She gave him a look then her eyes glanced down at his naked chest and he smiled. "Do you mean because I'll be sleeping in your bed, lass?"

The light by the fire was enough for him to see the blush on her cheeks and he chuckled, nuzzling her. "My sister will jump to the conclusion that the baby is mine and demand I marry you before she disowns me. If that doesn't work, she will follow me around the house and hit me with anything she can find."

Katrina smacked his chest. When he chuckled, she frowned and tried to squirm out from under him. "Lass, you really don't think I plan on keeping you as my mistress? When we get to my sister's, the preacher will marry us and we'll keep Arthur's identity a secret. He'll be our son."

The look on Katrina's face let him know she wasn't as pleased by the prospect of marrying him as he thought she would be. When she pushed on his shoulders, he obeyed and let her push him off her. He didn't understand why she was so upset. They had already slept together, she obviously enjoyed it. She was living with him, the only logical thing for them to do was marry. Protecting both her and the baby from being ostracized and adding protection to the infant that was being hunted, seemed like the right thing.

Katrina rolled away from him he followed her, touching her shoulder. Bryan was surprised when she stiffened under his touch. "I will not marry you."

Bryan was confused by her response. Katrina had been a virgin, so he knew she was not the type of lass to sleep around. She had been saving herself for her husband, which should be him. She agreed to stay with him and they were sleeping together, she should be happy he told her they were getting married.

"You will marry me," Bryan said, his voice coming out harsher than he meant.

He watched as Katrina turned her head and glanced at him over her shoulder giving him a look that let him know she was not going to budge. Before turning her back on him, she pulled the blankets up to her shoulders and dismissed him.

Bryan rolled onto his back, confused, as he watched as the firelight played on the ceiling. Katrina should be happy he was going to marry her. Bryan turned and looked at the back of her head and the blond hair on his pillow. He doubted she would appreciate that he was smiling at her. Even though he had no idea why she was suddenly mad, he still found her adorable.

He waited until he saw her body relax and heard her breathing even out. Bryan curled up behind her and wrapped his arm around her, wanting to hold her before he fell asleep. Katrina sighed and he felt her wiggle closer to him. Kissing the back of her head, Bryan smiled as he finally drifted off to sleep.

The next morning Bryan awoke just as Arthur started to make happy noises from his bed. He was a happy baby and slept most nights without waking up. He knew from his younger siblings and his sisters' new baby, that it wasn't always the case. Looking down, he saw Katrina lying across his chest. Her leg was tucked between his, her hand on his chest and he couldn't help but notice how small she was compared to him and how she fit him perfectly.

When Arthur started making more noises, he slid out from underneath her. Bryan picked up Arthur who let out a happy squeal. Bryan glanced at the bed, before walking out, admiring the vision that Katrina made with her hair across his pillow as she slept.

After cleaning and feeding Arthur, he laid him on his fur bed and watched as he cooed and made noises to get Snow's attention. Arthur kicked his feet as if trying to get the big wolf to stop pretending to be uninterested.

Bryan thought over the events of last night. Katrina telling him she wouldn't marry him wasn't an option. He knew she cared about him. Her telling him no made no sense. Any woman in her circumstances should be happy he wanted to marry her. What was she thinking?

Having sisters, Bryan thought he understood women. They were all happily married and glad to have kids of their own to raise. Katrina telling him no threw him for a loop. Hearing a noise from the room, he saw Katrina standing in the doorway.

"You should have woken me up," Katrina said as she stepped into the room noticing how Arthur kicked happily as she approached.

She bent down and picked him up, giggling when he grabbed her face. He tried to give her a big open mouth kiss and Katrina made a smacking noise while she let him. Bryan watched. He knew she was a lady and probably had little interactions with babies before this, but she seemed to grow more at ease every day.

Bryan stood and walked over to her then reached up to brush a stray blond hair back from her shoulder. He noticed the way Katrina tensed a bit at his touch and how she bit her lower lip. Bryan wanted nothing more than to kiss that lower lip.

Bryan opened his mouth to say something, anything, to ease the tension between them. Suddenly, Snow and the other wolves sat up at attention. Snow's lip curled, exposing his fangs as he growled and walked to the door.

All the wolves followed and Bryan went to the window to watch outside. He couldn't see anything but trusted them enough to know they had picked up on something. Bryan carefully opened the door, and the four wolves ran out, taking off into the woods so fast they were a flash of fur and then gone.

Bryan closed the door, and Katrina remained standing where he had left her, holding Arthur close to her chest. "What is it?"

"I don't know, lass, but we have to be prepared," Bryan said, grabbing her arms and gazing into her eyes. "I don't know what's coming, but I need you to promise me you'll listen to me when I tell you to do something, lass. Can you do that for me?"

Katrina nodded and Bryan gave in to the temptation that was before him and kissed her deeply. Arthur squirmed between them, letting out a sound that let them know he didn't appreciate being smothered. Bryan kissed the top of his head before letting her go.

Bryan led her to the back of the bedroom. Moving the chest, he showed her a small bolt hole. "This will get you out and into the bushes. If I tell you to leave, you go this way and try to go straight. There is a hill with a cave that you can hide in until I find you."

Katrina nodded and he tried to give her a smile. "Get a bag of things ready for you and Arthur just in case."

With a nod, Katrina went back to the front room. Bryan went to his chest of drawers and pulled out a small dagger. It was his mother's; his father had given it to her so she could protect herself when they traveled. His sisters each had their own and they had given it to him hoping he would give it to a woman when he decided to finally settle down. She might not have agreed to marry him yet, but she would, and now seemed like a good time to give her this to keep her safe.

CHAPTER 11

Katrina filled the two extra bladders full of milk, before wrapping up the hard cheese and bread. She didn't know if they would have to leave or not, but she knew that just in case, it was best to be prepared.

Had Morgana and her men found her and Arthur? The last time they attacked her, they killed all the Kings' guards, and the wolves and Bryan had saved them. Would they be able to save her again?

Feeling the panic begin to rise up inside her, she turned to see Bryan coming from the room, the light from the windows catching the blade in his hand. The thought of something happening to him made her heart stop. She loved him. Bryan had saved her and taken her in. Each morning he woke up and took care of Arthur for her, so she could sleep. He treated her differently than other men. Despite his large size, he was gentle and had taken in two wolves and earned their trust. Bryan was not like anyone she had ever met before.

When he walked up to her, she noticed he was frowning. "I want you to keep this on you," Bryan said, as he looked her over trying to figure out where on her dress he could possibly hide a dagger.

"I -- I don't know how to use one of those," Katrina said, taking a step back from him.

Bryan frowned, and she realized he must have come to the conclusion that there was nowhere on her dress that she could possibly hold that thing in his hand.

"Katrina, I will do my best to protect you, but if I fail..." his voice trailed off and she swallowed hard thinking about what he meant.

"If you want to marry me, you won't fail," Katrina said, blurting out the first thing that came to her head.

Bryan growled and pulled her into his arms. His mouth came down hard upon hers, his tongue thrusting inside her claiming her with a dominance he had never used before. Unable to help herself, she melted into him, her hands coming up and holding onto his shirt, as his tongue dueled with hers, laying claim.

When he broke the kiss, she slowly opened her eyes to find him breathing as hard as she was. "We are getting married, lass. I will not fail."

Bryan's words made her smile. She watched as he slid the dagger into the bag. "Put this by the bolt door and be prepared for anything."

She nodded and quickly went and placed the bag where he told her to. When she was done, she watched him as he pulled out a thick, leather shirt men wore during training from his bag he had kept near the door. It helped from piercing or stray arrows. It was light enough not to hinder his movement but added a layer of protection. After Bryan had put it on, she stepped up, putting her hand on his to stop him from trying to tie it.

"Let me," she whispered.

The shirt tied on the sides. One string was long enough to wrap around him and tied to the one in front. Doing this for

Bryan put her right up against his body. She blushed being so close to him. When she fell asleep last night, she was so angry at him for assuming what she wanted and not asking her, but at this moment all she could think about was, if they survived this, she would do anything he told her.

"Katrina," Bryan whispered, causing her to look up at him.

Their eyes locked and she blushed pulling the last string. Her hand on his side, he turned toward her and cupped her cheek. She leaned into his touch and closed her eyes. His lips brushed against hers, and she smiled.

"Come lass," Bryan said, as he took her hand and guided her to the window. "The wolves went in that direction. I need you to watch out this window. I need to see what is going on. If you see one shadow, of anything, you run out the bolt hole and head straight. Do you understand lass?"

Katrina nodded, blinking back tears. Before he could take a step back, she pressed her lips against his. It was a quick, hard kiss and when she broke it, she took a step back and her eyes met his. "Come back to me."

With a nod, he stepped from her, and she watched as he looked at Arthur before grabbing the quiver of arrows and his bow. Then, he strapped his sword to his back and walked out the front door. She watched as Bryan followed the trail the wolf took into the woods. She took a deep breath, got the dagger out of the bag he'd left for her and sat near the window. As she kept an eye out, she also said her prayers to the gods above to protect Bryan and keep her and Arthur safe.

CHAPTER 12

Every step Bryan took deeper into the woods was farther and farther away from Katrina and Arthur. His natural instinct was to stay with them but he knew if they reached the house, the chances of the two of them getting away got smaller.

Following the trail, Bryan saw when the wolves split up. He followed Snow knowing that as alpha of his small pack, he would be taking the most direct route and that his brother would be circling then coming up from behind on whoever had gotten their attention.

Bryan had only ever seen them act that way when they came across Morgana's men in the woods. It didn't take long before he heard the shouts of several men and the growl of his wolves. He carefully followed the sound. Stopping behind a tree, he grabbed an arrow and shot at one of the men rushing toward Snow with his blade high.

With one shot straight to his back, the man fell to the ground. He took aim and shot at the next man while trying to see how many of them were out there. Every time he heard one of the wolves growl, he saw more men appear and realized that the other three were forcing most of them from the woods, causing them to group up. There were so many of them, Bryan knew he wouldn't be able to stop them all on his own. All he could do was decrease the number and hopefully give Katrina and Arthur enough time to escape.

Bryan had shot several more arrows when he saw a man coming out of the woods. His arm was up and about to throw a dagger at him when he saw Minx jump out of the woods. She landed on him from behind, saving Bryan as her teeth bit the back of Morgana's man's neck.

Bryan started walking back, shooting arrows as he went when he felt someone come up behind him. He turned, grabbing the sword from his back, swinging it just in time to block the blow of the man sneaking up on him. Bryan was quickly able to gain an advantage and stabbed the man, killing him.

That was when he noticed that some of Morgana's men were already behind him. Taking aim, he shot the one farthest away before running after the one closest to him. Minx appeared at his side, and she jumped on the back of the man closest to them.

In front of him, he saw the leader, the same one from before. Bryan needed to warn Katrina so she could escape. With a whistle, he got Minx's attention and he pointed in the direction of the house. "Minx, protect!"

Minx took off in a flash heading toward the house. Bryan followed behind the men. The tattoos he had noticed on their faces ran the length of their back. Every one of them was shirtless with tattoos and piercings and the few he got close to had eyes that were almost completely black.

When he stopped the next one, Bryan felt a blade slice against his arm, cutting him. It wasn't deep enough to hinder his movement, so he swung high and hard, his sword was sharp enough to cut the head off with one stroke.

Time was not on his side and Bryan felt his panic rise, hoping against hope that Minx managed to warn Katrina in time to get out. When Bryan got to the house, the door was kicked open, none of Morgana's men were in sight. Bryan ran into the house and into his room. He sighed in relief when he saw the bolt door open.

Bryan ran out of the house grabbing the extra quiver of arrows he kept by the door. This was all he had left and based on how many of Morgana's men he saw earlier, it wouldn't be nearly enough. When he ran around to the back, he saw a very visible trail left by Katrina as she tried to run away. Between the dress and carrying Arthur, she would leave a trail even a blind man could follow, and he swallowed the lump in his throat as he saw the trail of men following her.

Scared, Katrina watched for what felt like hours, until she saw Minx run through the woods. Covered in blood, Katrina knew instantly that Bryan had sent her to warn her. She opened the door letting Minx in, as she ran to the back, grabbing Arthur and the bag that Bryan made her pack. She opened the bolt door, holding Arthur tight to her with one arm, as she gripped the blade with the other.

Minx walked in front of her, leading her out as Katrina started panicking about what was next. How far would she get holding Arthur? He was too big for her to carry in the bag and she knew it would soon be dark, and she didn't know if they would get that far.

Arthur started to fuss and she tried her best to sooth him while walking quickly. When she saw a large clearing, Katrina debated about what to do. The clearing was the fast way to get to the hill Bryan mentioned, but it also exposed her.

She noticed Arthur, who was still fussing in her arms, his lips quivering. "It's okay, Arthur. Bryan promised he would be right behind us."

Minx stayed beside her as she started to try to run as quickly as she could across the clearing. When Minx stopped and started growling, Katrina looked up to see a large man stepping from the trees. He was covered in tattoos and she felt his black eyes piercing her.

She held the dagger tighter taking a step back when she heard a sound behind her. She turned quickly and saw men coming up out of the woods. Every one of them shirtless, covered with tattoos and eyes as black as their leaders. Minx kept low in front of her and watched the leader as if she automatically knew who the biggest threat was.

"Give me the boy," the leader finally spoke, as he took a step toward her. His voice was deep with a thick accent that caused her to shudder. The setting sun seemed to shimmer off the giant battle ax he had strapped on his back, making the dagger in her hand look more like something one would use to eat with instead of protecting themselves.

"No," Katina managed to say with more conviction in her voice than she felt as she drew herself taller.

When the man laughed, everyone laughed with him. The echoing sound was chilling, which added to her fear. Minx stayed by her side and Katrina tried to find an opening. One of the men stepped forward and Minx bared her teeth as she crouched low. She was about to pounce on the man when a whistling sound passed by her ear, immediately followed by an arrow flying past her and landing in the leader's chest.

As she turned her head, she saw Bryan coming from the woods with the other three wolves in tow. He screamed a battle cry that echoed. The men all started to run toward her and Minx jumped on the closest one, quickly tearing at his throat. The other three wolves got to her before the men did and they kept a circle around her as Bryan fought his way to her.

With a quick stab, he killed the last man that was behind her as he came and stood inside the circle of wolves, who were keeping everyone from her. All of Morgana's men pulled out their swords and began to circle them again, this time closer.

Before they broke the circle, a flash of lightning appeared in the sky above them. Katrina screamed as the man in front of her got hit by a bolt of lightning. She looked around and saw Merlin standing at the opening, the air shimmering around him. He raised his hand and this time lightning flew from his fingers to the surrounding men, who began to attack. The wolves jumped first, but Bryan had pulled her behind him, telling her to stay close as chaos began to erupt all around them.

CHAPTER 13

Bryan swung his sword, killing the man in front of him, just in time to fend off the next attack. The sound of Arthur's cry was muffled by the sound of thunder that rolled overhead, as bolts of lightning streaked around him. He was never so surprised, or grateful, as when Merlin showed up.

The sound of one of the wolves crying in pain caught Bryan's attention. He turned just in time to see one of the men pulling out a sword from the wolf before kicking him away. Bryan turned when he heard Arthur's screams and saw Katrina struggling with one of the barbarians who was trying to rip Arthur from her arms. Before he could react, Katrina moved her hand and stabbed the man in the chest. The man staggered back but wasn't dead and Bryan quickly pulled her behind him as he stabbed him again.

When another group of men started to emerge from the woods, Bryan felt his heart sink, when suddenly Merlin shouted, "Down now!"

Bryan put his arm around Katrina and forcefully brought her down to her knees. He then put his body over hers, covering her from whatever was coming. Bryan kept his face down but felt the air all around them heat up, as Arthur's cries got louder. He worried that he might be squeezing Katrina and Arthur too hard but couldn't risk getting up.

As quickly as the rush of heat hit him, it was gone. He carefully looked up to see all the men lying on the ground dead. The wolves must have followed his lead as he saw Snow stand, first checking on his mate, Minx, licking her cheek. Bryan helped Katrina to her feet. Looking around, he only saw Merlin, slowly walking toward them. His eyes were glowing, neon-blue, so Bryan stood in front of Katrina.

Merlin nodded at him. "Take Katrina back to your home. I will be there shortly, after I make sure no one else comes for you."

Bryan nodded. He had many questions for Merlin, but they could wait. First, he needed to get Katrina back to their home and take care of Arthur, who was starting to fuss.

Katrina was pale, and her body was still shaking, reacting to everything she had just been through. The blade still held tightly in her hand, as it dripped with the blood of the man who had dared attack her. Very slowly, he put his hand over hers. "Katrina, I'm going to take you home now, okay? Can I have this?"

When she nodded, he took the dagger and slipped it into his belt. He gave her a gentle kiss before reaching out and taking Arthur from her. His free arm slid around her before he looked over to Snow's brother, who was lying on the ground trying to get up, while the other three wolves tried to help by nuzzling him.

"I'll take care of the wolves, they'll be fine," Merlin stated after Bryan hesitated, not wanting to leave his family behind.

Choosing to trust Merlin after he had saved them, he guided a shaking Katrina to the house. Arthur fussed quietly and put his thumb in his mouth. When he got to the house, he sat Katrina down before gently putting Arthur in her arms.

He didn't often drink, but he kept a bottle of scotch in his cupboard and poured her a small draft. He handed it to her and picked up Arthur trying to settle him while Katrina took a sip. If he weren't so worried about her, Katrina's response to the drink would have been comical because, her eyes widened, and her breath came out in a whoosh, then she started coughing.

Bryan watched as her color slowly returned. "Are you okay, lass?"

Katrina nodded, reaching for Arthur. "I think he is hungry."

Katrina opened her bag and got one of the bladders of milk and went to the room to feed him. Bryan wanted to follow her but felt she might need this time alone to come to terms with what had happened.

After a bit, he went and checked on Katrina. Not surprisingly, he found her asleep in the bed with Arthur. His finger brushed her cheek and he took the fur at the foot of the bed to cover her up. He stroked her cheek, smiling. She'd fought bravely to protect the baby sleeping soundly next to her.

Bryan went back to the front room to find Merlin inside. He didn't have to look around to know, that none of the wolves were there. Opening his mouth to ask where they were, Merlin put his hand up effectively silencing him. "They're in the stables. They'll be fine but need the rest."

"Do you want a drink?" Bryan asked sarcastically, when he noticed that Merlin had already gotten out two wooden cups and was pouring them both a scotch.

Merlin smiled, handing him one of the cups before motioning for him to sit. "When I sent Katrina from my home with the prince, I didn't realize Morgana's men were already after her. She must have had someone in the castle watching. The kingdom is forever in your debt for saving him and for what you're about to do."

Bryan raised an eyebrow. "What do you mean, *what I am about to do?*"

Merlin kept his gaze locked on him. "You and Katrina need

to leave. They will think that they found your bodies and the baby, burned in a fire with the others. Once that story starts to spread, you won't be able to stay here. The two of you need to leave."

Bryan wanted to argue, but there was nothing he could say. If he moved with his sister they would still be able to find the three of them and he would just be bringing trouble to his sister's door. When he opened his mouth to say something, Katrina stepped from the bedroom.

"I can go alone," She announced proudly.

"No lass, you promised to marry me and will not be going anywhere alone," Bryan said standing up to take her hand and pull her into the room.

"You have family Bryan, I could never ask you ––"

Bryan kissed her gently, effectively stopping her from finishing her sentence. When he pulled back, he smiled down at her. "Come lass, let's listen to what Merlin has to say."

Katrina nodded, and he helped her into the chair closest to him. Merlin gave Katrina a small smile before continuing. "I'm sorry Katrina. I didn't know things would come out the way they did. Morgana's grown stronger than even I was able to predict. I thought I had time to lead them away from you, but she found you first. Now, to keep the three of you safe, you must leave. The two of you must raise him as your child."

"He's the crown prince, can't we..." Katrina started to ask, the panic in her voice sneaking out.

Merlin shook his head, and Bryan reached out and took her hand. "Trust me Katrina, one day all will be revealed, but for now you must leave."

Merlin stood up and gave them a reassuring a smile. "Bryan, I'll be back in two days. Pack whatever you can't replace. The rest, leave here."

Bryan nodded and closed the door after Merlin left. He took a step toward Katrina, who was standing up wringing her hands.

"Lass, it'll be okay," Bryan said wrapping his arms around her and pulling her close, needing to hold her after the day's events.

Katrina looked up at him with tears in her eyes. "What if I'm not?"

Bryan stopped her words with a quick kiss trying to stop her from thinking that way. He broke the kiss and brushed the hair back from her face. "Together we are."

Katrina nodded and he knew in his heart those words were true. Together, they would leave and raise the crown prince in secret. He also knew that one day they would need to come back. But, for now, their job was to hide Arthur and keep him safe, so when he got old enough, strong enough, he could come home and take back his kingdom.

ABOUT THE AUTHOR

Leilani Love is a USA Today Best selling author and Gold Medal Winner of the Readers Favorite Paranormal Books 2016.

    A proud mother of two very active boys. She loves traveling to new places and meeting new people wherever she goes. Thus far, Leilani has visited Paris, DenBosch and Amsterdam and hopes to one day return. On her next trip she hopes to be able to make stops in Scotland and Italy. Currently residing in Oregon, she has also lived in Hawaii, Florida, Alaska, Virginia, Texas, Washington and California. She loves to read books and has a passion for various genres. Her love affair with dragons began when she was young and she still dreams of having her own dragon and Black Panther. For now, she is content to write about them in her books.

SNEAK PEEK THE LOST KING ~ A KING'S TALE

Colley called down to Arthur as he walked out of the Madam's house. Arthur turned and winked up at her as she leaned out the window, a flirty grin on her lips and her breast spilling out of the frayed red robe she'd put on after he left.

"Arthur, you come back real soon, and ask for me," she cooed, before she blew him a kiss.

Arthur's chest puffed up with pride as he winked at her, then he stepped back and bowed. Once he straightened, he noticed that one of the women he had met briefly downstairs was now in the window next to Colley. "Next time you come Arthur, Colley will have to quit being so selfish and let the rest of us have a go." With that, she stood up and parted her robe, baring her overly large breasts for the world to see. His eyes widened in appreciation. As he took another step back, he slipped on a pile of mud and landed on his back with a plop.

His eyes closed as he tried to catch his breath. The sound of laughter from Colley and her friend forced him to open his eyes and look up to find a woman as lovely as the famed goddess Venus peering down. She was wearing a white fur cloak that covered her from the neck down. As his gaze scanned up, he noticed perfectly shaped, bow lips quirked up into a soft smile. When his gaze finally met hers, he found himself getting lost in a pair of slanted, sapphire blue eyes framed by thick, long lashes. One of her brows arched up in amusement and her midnight black hair had two perfect ringlets that framed her lovely face.

Still trying to catch his breath he opened his mouth, but no words came out as he watched her turn her head and look up to the windows above. Her cheeks flushed a lovely shade of pink and she quickly averted her gaze. A quick glance showed him that Colley had chosen not to be outdone by her friend, and Arthur blushed trying to get up to apologize.

Before he could get to his knees, a giant of a man appeared behind her and whispered something in her ear, making her nod and walk away from him. He followed her with his gaze as she walked to a carriage, and the giant man talked to the driver. A little boy no older than five years came running past and grabbed something from her cloak. Before he could yell, the mountain man grabbed the kid and held him in the air by the collar of his shirt.

He gave the child a sympathetic look as the goddess walked up to him and placed her hand on his arm. Too far away to hear what was being said, he watched as they exchanged words until the boy pointed to a nearby shop. The blonde woman who had been standing near the carriage door gave the giant a nod and disappeared to where the boy pointed, and then reappeared from the corner with a younger girl who was covered in more mud than the street he was lying in.

The man set the boy on his feet and kept a hand on his collar, so that he couldn't run. The dark-haired Venus opened the door to the carriage and the giant man swore under his breath and used his free hand to help her in before he picked up both children and put them inside the carriage. The lady's blonde companion was grinning away as he helped her, and he could see the man's irritation by his stiff jaw and jerky movements. He couldn't hear what the man was muttering but if he were a betting man the words were not fit for mixed company.

Arthur wished he was close enough to hear what had just happened and where she was taking the kids. When he stood up, he noticed a man who looked to be chuckling at the scenario that had just happened. "Who was that?" Arthur asked hoping the man knew.

"That was Princess Guinevere," the man said as he walked toward him. The big smile he gave Arthur showed his dimple on his right cheek. His hazel eyes danced with mischief and his wavy hair blew out around his face.

There was something about him. Arthur was curious about the man, but more so about the woman who'd just left. "Princess Guinevere? The one who is expected to marry the crown prince?"

The man gave a short nod, "The one and only."

Arthur turned to look as the carriage started to leave and the children were no longer in sight. "Did she just kidnap those two children?"

The man laughed. "It depends on whom you ask, some say she kidnaps them and bathes in their blood for beauty, others say she rescues them."

Arthur shook his head. He had heard rumors about the Princess Guinevere, but he never could have imagined she would appear before him like a goddess He heard his cousin Lancelot chuckle as he walked up behind him and clasped him on his back, "She is way above you, cousin. You have a better chance of sleeping with the queen herself than getting near the Ice Princess."

When Arthur turned around again, the man had vanished. "I don't know about that dear friend."

∽

Guinevere tried not to smile as Bors gave her a dirty look. His brown eyes narrowed as he took the young girl from Elizabeth. Elizabeth was Bors' only daughter, and her companion and she also appeared to be having a hard time not laughing at the situation.

"Milady, you can't rescue every thief you find on the street," Bors said, giving her a stern look even as he reached into his bag to give both children a piece of bread.

It tugged at her heart to see the young boy only take a few bites so that his little sister could have more. "Bors, they are hungry. We couldn't leave them out there." She leaned forward in the seat and gave the boy another slice of bread. "What is your name?"

"Marcus," he whispered.

When the little girl yawned, she tried to sit on her brother's lap. Bors grumpily pulled her from her brothers lap and tucked her onto his own. Marcus looked like he wanted to complain, but then his sister looked up at the giant of a man who held her and curled up closer to him before closing her eyes. Marcus sat back but kept a wary eye on the man.

"Marcus, can I have my purse back?" she asked, reaching out her hand.

With a swallow, he reached into his sleeve and pulled it out, handing it to her. "You have very quick fingers Marcus, I almost didn't feel it."

"I—I am sorry," he stuttered.

"Where is your mother? Your father?" she asked, curious.

"They passed," Marcus answered as he looked down.

Guinevere nodded. Lately there had been more and more orphaned children. Bors often accused her of trying to save them all. She sat back in her seat and avoided looking at Bors. Despite all his complaining, she knew he would never leave the children out there alone. Elizabeth pretended to be busy, but Guinevere could almost feel her smiling.

"Milady, what are we going to say to the Prince when we show up with two children?" Bors asked, as he adjusted the girl in his arms, so she could rest comfortably.

Guinevere sighed. He was right. Prince Greggory was known for a lot of things, but his generosity and love for his people was definitely not one of them. Guinevere was here visiting with Greggory and his family. The last discussion of when her and Greggory's wedding would take place resulted in a promise from her father that she would spend more time at Camelot. It looked like her father's attempts to stall the wedding were causing a rift, and Guinevere knew that soon she would be forced to fulfill the obligation of her wedding contract.

Not one to wallow in self-pity, she looked at the boy and the little girl across from her sleeping soundly on Bors. "Before we get to the castle, there is a widow who lives outside. We can stop by her house and drop the children off there. Give her some money to clothe and feed them, we'll have her keep an eye on them until we can figure out what to do."

Bors nodded and Guinevere stared out the window. When they neared the widow's house, Bors tapped on the carriage wall, telling the driver to stop. They had been to the widow's house enough that the driver must have guessed what she wanted and pulled up to the house. Bors' hands were full of the two sleeping children, so the driver opened the door and helped Guinevere out. When he took her hand, she gave him a bright smile, "Thank you."

Murphy's cheek turned bright red and he bobbed his head, "You're welcome, milady."

Guinevere took a step forward as she straightened her dress. The widow's name was MaryAnn and she had two children of her own. They were older, ten and twelve, if she remembered correctly. They'd met when the two boys had decided to run in front of a carriage that she was in with the Prince. Since the Prince was driving his new open carriage, he wanted to teach the boys a lesson. MaryAnn had come out begging him to show mercy and Guinevere herself talked him out of the lashing he'd decided they deserved.

MaryAnn stepped from the cabin, giving her a warm, welcoming smile. When she started to bow Guinevere quickly took a step forward taking her hand in hers to stop her. "MaryAnn, I was wondering if I could impose on you to do me a favor."

"Anything Your Highness," she said, nodding eagerly.

"This is Marcus and his sister. Would you mind helping by keeping them with you until I can find them a home?" Guinevere asked as Bors helped the sleepy boy down while still holding Marcus' little sister in his arms.

"It will be an honor, milady."

Bors helped her bring them in and Elizabeth paid her several gold coins. Guinevere took MaryAnn's hand smiling, "Thank you so much for your help."

MaryAnn blushed, nodding, "You saved my boys and have helped my family so much. I owe you so much more than just watching over two children who look like they need some motherly care. If you need anything else, please don't hesitate to ask."

Guinevere nodded and let Bors lead her back into the carriage, fussing over her like an old mother hen as he told her that they were running late. Sitting properly in her spot, she adjusted her dress and looked out the window, wishing there was something else she could do for her people besides honoring a contract her father had signed with the previous king. She wished he'd never signed it. How could he have promised her to a man before either of them had even been born?

VIOLCA'S DRAGON ~ THE DRAGON RUBY SERIES

Shooting up in her bed, Violca reached for her throat, feeling for any cuts or bruises. She knew rationally that nothing would be there, even as her heart continued to pound and her breath came in short pants.

The soft squeak of the door drew Violca's attention. It had opened just enough for her youngest sister, Angyalka to peek her head in. Her sister's name was Hungarian for Angel. She was born with hair so pale blonde that it looked like she was born with a halo. Her mother had teased that she would either be an angel or the devil in disguise. Out of all the girls she was the one who looked most like their father. The rest of the sisters had dark hair, just like their mother. "Hey Angel, what're you doing up?" Violca asked, patting the bed next to her.

At ten, Angyalka still loved to cuddle with her. "I heard you scream," she announced as she quickly crawled into the bed.

Running her fingers through her little sister's hair, she saw her lip quiver as she made this little statement. Since their parents' death two years back, Violca had been raising her four sisters, in large part thanks to the life insurance policy their parents left. It helped that they owned a four-bedroom house which did not require too much upkeep.

Violca had dropped out of college and taken on a full-time job as a receptionist in a law office, just to make sure she would be home nights with her sisters. Angyalka, being so young, often clung to her, and she felt her heart tighten at the obvious fear in her sister's voice. "It was just a bad dream, sweetie. I'm okay, I promise." Feeling her sister curl up closer to her side she added, "Why don't you stay with me tonight and help keep the bad dreams away?"

"Okay," Angyalka mumbled while snuggling under the covers and putting her head down on the pillow.

Kissing her sister on the forehead, Violca lay down next to her and curled her arms around her. Angyalka quickly fell asleep. Listening to the slow rhythmic sound of her sister's breathing helped pull Violca back into sleep.

The alarm went off at 5:30 a.m. and she quickly turned it off, hoping not to wake up her sister as she got out of bed to hop in the shower. She still felt groggy, since her sleep had been interrupted, but she was thankful that after her sister had climbed into bed with her, the dreams had left her alone for the rest of the night.

Feeling the hot water run down her body, Violca couldn't help but think of her dream about her mother. While heading out for their 25th wedding anniversary, their parents were hit by a car that ran a red light. Last night was the first time she had dreamt of her mother in over a year, and even though she knew it was just a dream, she couldn't help but wish her mother could talk to her. Violca had at first felt so overwhelmed when she'd started taking care of her sisters, but they were a family and nothing was going to keep them apart.

Stepping out of the shower, Violca wrapped the towel around her body and blow dried her hair. While all the sisters, except Angyalka, had their mother's jet-black hair, Violca was the only one with their mother's violet eyes, giving her the name Violca, Hungarian for Violet. The other girls were all born with their dad's sparkling blue eyes. Finishing with her hair, Violca applied the bare minimum of makeup, lipstick, eye shadow, and mascara as she proceeded to finish her routine, so she could get the girls' breakfasts ready.

Walking into the kitchen, she saw that the girls were already up. Sari, the second youngest, was standing behind Angyalka, doing her hair in a light braid. They were the closest, being the youngest two, and they always seemed to be whispering to each other. Kati was washing fruit in the sink, and Eva was getting the bread out for sandwiches.

Taking out the pancake mix, Violca noticed one of her sisters had already turned on the griddle, and she started mixing. "Hey guys, you all got your homework done. Right?"

"Of course, V. I've got a party this weekend, and I know you won't let me go if I slack off," Eva answered. Eva was seventeen and a senior this year. She was constantly being invited to parties. Since she was the second oldest, she helped the most. As soon as she was able to drive, she had taken their father's old Corolla and helped with transporting the kids, mainly taking them to school or running errands while Violca was still at work.

Angyalka and Sari both answered simultaneously, "Yes, we finished early so we could watch cartoons."

Violca looked over at Kati, who gave her a half smile and nodded, yes. Out of all the girls, Kati was the quietest, keeping to herself. She was fifteen years old, about to turn sixteen, and Violca knew this was a rough time for her. She had a quiet strength and her blue eyes showed wisdom beyond her years.

While passing out the pancakes, Violca couldn't help but wish her parents could see how the girls were turning out. All of them were doing well in school and excelling in their own areas. Sitting down, she listened to the girls talk about what they had planned and who needed to do what. Not much for talking in the morning, she enjoyed the sounds of their laughter and the chatter that just seemed to be a natural part of their lives.

Printed in the USA
CPSIA information can be obtained
at www.ICGtesting.com
CBHW022040240524
8976CB00004B/72